SACRED MONSTER

DONALD E. WESTLAKE

SACRED MONSTER

THE MYSTERIOUS PRESS

New York • London • Tokyo

The Mysterious Press, 129 West 56th Street, New York, N.Y. 10019

Printed in the United States of America

First Printing: May 1989

10 9 8 7 6 5 4 3 2 1

Library of Congress Cataloging-in-Publication Data

Westlake, Donald E.
    Sacred monster.

    I. Title.
PS3573.E9S23   1989   813'.54   88-28888
ISBN 0-89296-177-5

With sympathy and respect, this novel is dedicated to the memory of (in alphabetical order):

        Esther Blodgett
        Daisy Clover
        Norma Desmond
        Emily Ann Faulkner
        and
        Georgia Lorrison

SACRED MONSTER

"This won't take long, sir."

Oooooooooooooooooohooooooooooooooooooooooooooooohoo ooooooooooooooooooooooooohooooooooooooooooooooooooooh ooooooooooooooooooooooooooooooooooooooooooooooohooo ooooooooooooooooooooooooooooooooooooo, wow.

I hurt all over. My *bones* ache. God's giant fists are squeezing my internal organs, twisting and grinding. Why do I *do* it, if it makes me sick?

"Ready for a few questions, sir?"

I open my eyes; slowly, very slowly. It is daytime, but thank God a high, thin cloud cover shields me from the sun. I am home; where else would I be? Here is my broad slate patio, grayer than the thin cloud way up above, spread like a monochrome quilt between my house and my pool. Big house; white; Tara, you know what I mean? I can't look at the pool; dancing waters.

And ahead of me is the interviewer. A neat, drab man, a plain man in plain gray slacks, plain tan sports jacket, button-down blue shirt, maroon bow tie. Brown loafers, black socks. Steno pad at the ready, ball-point pen at the ready, eyes at the ready.

1

I open my mouth, which alters the balance of my body, which makes me dizzy, which makes me want to return to sweet oblivion. But duty calls. "Sure, pal," my voice says, with some assistance from me. "Anything for the press."

"Thank you," the interviewer says, neat and polite. He has a round, neat head without flab or jowls or character at all. No lumpy nose, thick lips, shaggy eyebrows, big ears. Nothing. Not a character you can catch *hold* of. He has a head like a shaved coconut with a seedy, flat wig pasted on.

Which is why he's a reporter and I'm a star. *I* am interesting. Even when I'm—oh, God! in *pain!*— I'm interesting. I mean, here he is, you see what I mean, pen and pad in hand, interested in *me*, while I don't give a fat rat's ass about *him*. You see how it works?

Well, no, let's be fair. It isn't just the face, this interestingly mottled and cunningly cragged visage the world has grown over the years to know and to love and to pay money for the sight of. Behind the face there's—there was—there *is*, dammit!—well, there was, anyway—a talent that would knock your socks off and tan your toes. This face, this voice . . . the slope of this shoulder, the movement of these hands . . .

I could still do it, if I had to. You don't think so? I could. I don't have to, of course, haven't had to for a long time, but I *still could*, if push came to goddamn shove. Still could.

Not today, however. Today I'm doing well enough just to sketch in the vaguest outline of a human being here. I risk disembowelment, self-destruction, by making a smile in my interviewer's direction, using all those *muscles* in the *face*. I say, "Where would I be without the press, huh?"

"I guess that's right," he says. He's so toneless I may die; I'm suffering life deprivation.

In fact, I'm *suffering*. "Listen, pal," I say, my voice waving and shaking all on its own, "I'm sorry, but I got really wasted last night. I took chemicals science hasn't discovered yet. I mean I just got back to this solar system, you follow me? I'm sorry, pal, but I just got to sit down."

2

He looks at me with faint concern. "Sir," he says, "you are sitting down."

I gaze about me in mild amaze. Son of a bitch, the man speaks true! Blue canvas cups my penitent rump. A pale blue terry-cloth robe is closed over legs stretching away from me over the slates, ankles crossed, feet bare but wonderfully clean. I am a clean person.

But sick. "In that case," I say, leaning forward, stretching out these arms, these arms, "in that case," tipping over my own knees, palms brushing slate, canvas chair groaning as I depart, "in that case, I got to *lie* down."

And so I do, stretching out on my back, the coolness of the slate filtering through the terry cloth to soothe my fevered ass, my sacrificial shoulder blades. My right hand comes up, knowing the appropriate gesture all by itself, the back of the hand resting on my forehead, fingers slightly curled. I gaze up past this monument at the herringbone sky. I speak:

"It is true that I am rich and famous. The movies I star in have never grossed less than eighty million. I make so much money I'm an *industry*. I support entire villages of lawyers and agents and managers and secretaries and accountants and hookers and dope dealers and plastic surgeons and ex-wives and relatives and friends and gardeners and poolmen and gym instructors. I've got people to stand me up when it is absolutely necessary that I stand up, to dry me out and clean me off when I must go once again in front of that old debbil camera, people to keep me out of trouble with the law, to buy me the very *best* dope money can buy. These people don't just love me, man, they *need* me."

I smile, thinking of my citizens. Delicately, carefully, I turn my head just enough to include the interviewer in my smile. "Jack Pine's army," I say.

"Yes, sir."

"But probably you want to know how it all began, am I right?"

"Yes, sir, I would," he says.

3

"How a God-given talent became such a far-flung enter-
prise."

I gaze again heavenward, thinking back . . .

*screams, screaming, engine roars, flashing lights in red
and white reflecting from the bumper chrome, slicking on the
heaving trunk of the car, madness, danger, movement, peril,
speed . . .*

No! I blink, I make some sort of noise out of my throat,
I press the back of my head against the hard slate, my
fingers clench at air. I will *not* let that in!

It's all right. It's all right. "Yes," I say, nodding, catching
hold of the reins once more. I smile. The practiced sentences roll forth: "It all began, it all began, the night I lost
my virginity."

She was my first. Wendy. Of course, I wasn't *her* first. Not even that night. But she was really nice. Really nice.

We went to the same school, she was a year behind me. I was sixteen, Wendy was fifteen, she went sometimes with three, four guys in a car. Her father's car. I heard about it, but I never thought she'd do it with *me*.

Buddy fixed it up, Buddy Pal, he set the whole thing up, just the two of us and Wendy. And naturally, because he set it up with Wendy, he went first.

FLASHBACK 1

Frank William Pal, Jr., known as Buddy, smiled at Wendy and backed out of the car. With the door open, the interior light had come on, and Wendy shielded her eyes with a pudgy-fingered hand. Supine on the backseat, blue jeans and panties in a snarl around her right ankle on the floor, sweater and bra bunched up to her armpits, she was less pretty but more provocative than when seen in the corridors at school, prancing along, eyes wise with knowing sidelong glances, lips full and mouth pink when she laughed. Now she breathed in little gasps, her pale belly contracting, and her voice was hoarse as she said, "Ow. Shut the door, willya?"

"I'll send Jack over," Buddy told her, and shut the door, killing the light. It was a soft and humid spring night, and the car windows were all steamed on the inside, making them opaque in the darkness. Buddy, a skinny six-footer of sixteen with nondescript brown hair, took the roll of paper towels he'd left on the car roof, ripped off a few, and put the roll back on the roof. After using the towels, he pulled his pants up, secured them, stepped into his loafers, and walked away from the dark and silent Buick, down the dirt road among the pine trees in the dark.

Jack Pine stood nervously walking and skipping and kicking at stones about a hundred feet down the road. He too was skinny at sixteen, his brown hair less controlled than Buddy's. They were similar in looks and build, enough so that people sometimes thought they might be cousins, but they were merely best friends. Their differences were not in their features, but what they did with them: Buddy's expressions were confident, amused, aware, while Jack's face mostly mirrored doubt and insecurity. Between the two, Buddy seemed the older, the more mature. He came strolling down the dirt road, smiling, hands in trouser pockets, and softly called, "Dad? You there?"

"Buddy? Here I am!" Jack's voice, anxious, was too loud, the words too jumbled together.

Buddy found him in the dark, and squeezed his arm. "Take it easy, Dad."

"I'm fine!" Jack told him, smiling maniacally though they could barely see each other. "Is Wendy—?"

"All softened up for you, Dad."

Jack swallowed. "I just—I just go over there?"

"She's waiting, Dad. You know what I mean? *Waiting.*"

"But—I don't know how to . . ." Jack's hands fluttered in the night like moths. "How to *act*. I don't know how to *act*."

"Act like me, Dad," Buddy told him, grinning as he presented the gift. "Just go over there and be me."

Jack's eyes widened. He looked at his friend as though for the first time. "I could," he whispered, awed by it.

"Sure, you could, Dad. Go on, get over there before she cools off."

Buddy gave him a little push, and Jack stepped toward the unseen Buick, tripping but recovering, moving on. In the dark, his movements were like Buddy's, gliding, insinuating, certain. Then he stopped and looked back. Above, clouds shifted, and the sheen of perspiration on Jack's face

7

suddenly gleamed pale in moonlight. His smile was one he'd never owned before. "Buddy?" he called, transfixed, spotlit by the moon. "Thanks!" And he turned away, sliding Buddy-like through the dark.

I smile at the sky, remembering that incredible moment, that instant when I opened the Buick's door and the light went on—like a movie starting, like a curtain going up on a play—and there she was, like nothing I'd ever seen before. And she held her arms out to me. . . .

I held my arms out, up, to the sky, the way I did when I played the Aztec prince. Red. There's blood on my hand, my right hand. Dried, dark, dull. I put my hand to my mouth, I lick the blood away. All gone. No evidence left. No matter. I forget all about it. "That was something," I say, living nothing but that first moment so long ago. "It was so exciting. My very first time. I just lost . . . I just lost all control. It was like an *explosion*. That's when I really and truly came to life."

From the corner of my eye, I see the interviewer make a note. A sexual suggestion, but just a hint, will get into his copy, past his editor. It's all good for my image. Then he looks at me and says, "Buddy Pal was there even back then, was he?"

"Oh, yeah," I say. "Buddy Pal's not only my best friend in all the world, he's my *oldest* friend in all the world. We met in *nursery school*, man. We ate *sand* together. And on to college."

FLASHBACK 2

In the college auditorium, in the evening, a production of *Hamlet* was being rehearsed. The director was a member of the school faculty, but all the actors were students. Act V, scene i, was being run through, in costume, but without scenery or sets.

The two gravediggers shuffled onto the bare stage, dressed in rags, shovels over their shoulders. The first gravedigger was a large and bulky boy of nineteen, moving like a football player at the end of a hard game, his manner awkward but willing. The second gravedigger, stepping slyly, hunch-shouldered, bowlegged, completely comfortable, was Jack.

The football player spoke first, in a flat monotone, like the telephone company announcing the time: "'Is she to be buried in Christian burial that wilfully seeks her own salvation?'" He gazed out over the dark auditorium as he declaimed, over the heads of the other actors and their friends and the jaundiced-looking director. He seemed unaware of the other person on stage, to whom he was allegedly speaking.

Jack shuffled around him, quick but obscurely infirm. His voice was a triumphant cackle as he said, "'I tell thee she is; and therefore make her grave straight.'" He winked and leered at his partner, sharing the joke with him, though the partner gave him nothing back. With mock solemnity, Jack crossed himself and sardonically intoned, "'The crowner hath sate on her, and finds it Christian burial.'" An echo of brogue lilted his speech.

"'How can that be,'" the football player said, one word thudding after another, "'unless she drown'd herself in her own defence?'"

Jack capered slightly, an arthritic imitation of a jester. "'Why, 'tis found so,'" he said, and winked.

The football player massively shook his head; acting. "'It must be *say often-dough*,'" he announced. "'It cannot be else. For here—'"

"*Wait* a minute!" called the director, rising from his front-row seat, hurrying up onto the stage. A balding, potbellied man of fifty, he was famous in the school for long brooding silences followed by excessive explosions followed by tortured apologies. While everyone else in the seats watched with half smiles of anticipation, this man crossed the stage to Jack and the football player, crying out, "What is this '*often-dough*'?"

"I dunno," the football player said, blinking and looking defensive. "That's what it says in the book."

"It is *not*," the director assured him, and waved a paperback copy under the football player's nose. "The phrase is '*se offendendo*.' Do you suppose you can say that?"

While the football player made a stumbling attempt to repeat the phrase, Jack looked toward the wings and saw Buddy there, just out of sight behind the side curtain, gesturing to Jack to come over. As the director attempted to teach *se offendendo* to the football player, with increasingly caustic asides, Jack crossed to the wings, walking with his usual quick buoyance, the shovel now jauntily borne on his shoulder. "Hi, Buddy," he said when he had cleared the stage.

Buddy spoke quietly, conspiratorially. "Listen, Dad," he said, "you stuck here?"

Jack smiled, like sunlight breaking through clouds. The hand not holding the shovel moved in an expansive delighted gesture. "I *love* it, Buddy! I'm alive here!"

Buddy nodded, without interest. "Oh, yeah?"

"Acting!" Jack beamed at the stage, where director and football player moved even further from understanding. "This is it for me," he said.

"Yeah, well, I got a date with that Linda from seventeenth-century lit."

Happy for his friend, Jack said, "Yeah? Great. She's okay!"

"Only I need a couple bucks, Dad," Buddy said. "Five?"

"Oh, sure, Buddy!"

Putting down the shovel, Jack searched his rags for his wallet, found it, and handed Buddy a bill. Buddy took it without comment, stowed it away in a pocket, and said, "Maybe she's got a pal for you, if you ever get outa here." Grinning, teasing with a little conspiratorial wink, he added, "And *if* you behave yourself."

Suddenly sheepish, Jack fiddled with the shovel, moving it from hand to hand. "*I* know how to handle girls," he said.

With an ironic laugh, Buddy said, "*Yes*, you do."

From the stage, the director, with a thin, high-nettled whine in his voice, called, "*Mister* Pine, could you manage to rejoin us, do you suppose?"

"Oh, sure!" Shouldering his shovel, Jack grinned at Buddy, said, "Luck with Linda," and hurried back to the middle of the stage, facing the exasperated director with his sunniest and most amiable smile. "Sorry," he said. "Here I am."

"So I see. We're going to try reversing the roles. You know the lines?"

"Oh, sure I do," Jack said. "They're all my cues."

"I don't," said the football player. He was now reduced to smoldering resentment.

"You'll read," the director told him, pushing the paper-

13

back into the football player's midsection. The football player took it like a handoff. The director gave them both an arch look, said, "From the top," and returned to his seat in the auditorium.

Jack and the football player left the stage; Buddy was already gone. After a moment they re-entered, this time Jack in front. The football player was stiffer than before, sullen anger visible in his expression and posture. This time, Jack was primmer, fussier. He kept smoothing and tidying the rags he wore. There was a hint of pursed-lipped pickiness in his expression and manner, and he sounded aggrieved when he said, "'Is she to be buried in Christian burial that wilfully seeks her own salvation?'"

"'I tell thee she is,'" the football player read, one word at a time, "'and therefore make her grave straight. The crowner hath sate on her, and finds it Christian burial.'"

"'How can that be,'" Jack demanded, taking personal affront, "'unless she drown'd herself in her own defence?'"

"'Why, 'tis found so,'" read the football player.

Jack was baffled by this. He took the shovel from his shoulder and stood it on the floor, then leaned on it, thinking the situation over. Shaking his head, he said, "'It must be *se offendendo*; it cannot be else.'" He turned so that the shovel stood between himself and the football player, then treated the shovel as though it were a lectern and he the lecturer. "'For here lies the point,'" he told the unlistening football player. "'If I drown myself wittingly, it argues an act; and an act hath three branches—it is, to act, to do, and to perform; argal, she drown'd herself wittingly.'" Having proved the point to his satisfaction, he released the shovel and spread both hands in accomplishment. The shovel stood poised, then began to topple, then was caught by Jack with a flowing movement that picked it up and placed it back on his shoulder.

The football player read, "'Nay, but hear you— '"

"Hold it!" cried the director from the auditorium. He was on his feet again, coming now to the edge of the stage, looking up at his actors, saying, "That's it, we'll keep it that way. You," he said, gesturing at Jack, "come here."

Jack went over to the edge of the stage, carrying the shovel on his shoulder. He went down on one knee, looking down at the director, saying, "Yes, sir?"

Quietly, but smiling, the director said, "You'll have to carry him, you know."

"Oh, he'll be fine," Jack said.

"Uh-huh. I wish I could have you play both parts," the director said.

Oh, how long have I been here? I'm all curled in a ball on the gray slate patio. When did I stop talking? Slowly, with a degree of pain, I straighten out of the fetal position, I lie straight again, on my back, legs straight, feet together, eyes staring up at the sky. White, blue, faded, faint, far-receding sky . . . Is someone screaming?

"So you knew right then you were an actor."

The interviewer's voice brings me back, his words make me happy. "Yes!" I say. "It *had* to be. I could feel it like, like, like chicken soup. Well, later, like bourbon. Like nose candy, you know what I mean?"

"It made you strong."

"It *flowed* through me," I say, feeling it again, the finest high there is. "It was warm, it was beautiful. Give me a role to play, give me the costume, give me the lines. I don't need an audience. That's why I'm good in the flicks, see? You got these stage actors who *need* that boost, that audience out there with that reaction right *now*, but I never did. I could play in a closet, man, just me and the coats, in the dark. Just give me somebody to *be*."

FLASHBACK 3

It was a cold and drizzly day in Grover's Corners, the needle-thin rain pasting trash and candy wrappers to the cement of street and sidewalk, the passing traffic a monotonous symphony of *shashing* tires and *flwacking* windshield wipers. Beside the big, lumpy blacktop parking lot with its few wet, mud-streaked automobiles like minor artifacts of a preceding civilization, the small building was incongruously bright and exuberant, with its impermeable pale green aluminum siding and the red neon bus-company name dominating its picture window. Posters and other signs cluttered that window with high-pitched come-ons: ski vacations, reliable taxi services, guaranteed package delivery, all-inclusive tours. Here in this false little building, fevered outside, grimy within, here nevertheless there stood the magic doorway between Grover's Corners and the world. Step through, or stay at home; no one can do both.

Inside, Jack and Buddy, both twenty-one, stood looking out, through the runnels of rain, waiting for their separate buses. They'd talked themselves out. Expectation, bravado, doubt, and then apprehension had each moved in its turn through their minds and speeches and expressions of face, leaving them now drained, emptied, waiting for a world of new experience to refill them. The only remaining residue of emotion was a faint embarrassment, a hint of premature homesickness, causing an inability to speak or to stand naturally, an unwillingness to meet each other's eyes for more than a glancing second before the gaze of each would slide away, back to the window, the rain, the inactive parking lot, the anonymous traffic on Main Street.

A bus appeared, out there, beyond the nearer line of traffic, signaling hugely for a left turn with a powerful and slowly blinking yellow light—the only vibrantly alive point in all that gray outdoors. The bus's huge windshield wipers moved vertically back and forth arrhythmically, to separate patterns, narrow straight-standing sentries patrolling to different beats.

Jack made a sound, then cleared his throat. He said, "Yours, or mine?"

"What dif?"

Both stood hipshot, palms against backs, fingers jammed down into hip pockets, in unconscious imitation of the calm insouciance of characters in westerns, but with angular tension in their poses. More than ever, that false familial similarity hovered over them.

A break in the streaming traffic; the bus made the turn, massively, arthritically, the fat driver visible in his rainy fishbowl, turning and turning the huge flat wheel. CHICAGO, said the sign above the windshield: Buddy's bus.

Jack's grin was spastic; he'd wanted it to be *his* bus. "Well, Buddy," he said, "you're on."

"Here I go," Buddy said, looking around for his single small suitcase. He saw it, pointed at it, but didn't pick it up yet. Just beyond the window, the bus heaved to a stop with a great hissing of air brakes. Passengers began to disembark. Buddy grinned at Jack. "Knock 'em dead, Dad," he said.

"You, too, Buddy."

Buddy's grin widened. "Well, sure," he said, and mimed spraying the interior of the depot with a machine gun.

Ex-passengers leaped the wet space from bus to depot doorway. Jack said, "I'll miss you."

"We'll both be around," Buddy said with a shrug. "Send my folks your address when you get to Big Town."

"Sure. And I'll get yours."

Buddy took a pack of cigarettes from his shirt pocket, shook out two, gave one to Jack. Jack brought a Zippo lighter from his trouser pocket and started to light Buddy's cigarette, but Buddy took the lighter out of his hand and lit both cigarettes. Then Buddy held the lighter up, flame off. He grinned at Jack and closed his hand around the lighter, saying, "To remember you by, huh, Dad?"

There was just the slightest, tiniest hesitation, and then Jack became effusively agreeable: "Oh, sure! Take it, Buddy, sure thing. What a good idea. I should have thought of it myself."

"Fine," Buddy said, and pocketed the lighter, as outside the Chicago bus gave an irritable-sounding *honk*.

"Well," Jack said, suddenly exuding nervousness, "I guess you're off."

"Right." Buddy picked up his suitcase and grinned again. "Don't do anything I wouldn't do, Dad."

Awkwardly trying for a joke, Jack said, "Gives me plenty of leeway, huh?"

"That's right."

The two friends shook hands, firmly, smiling at each other. Then Buddy stepped out the door, ignored the rain, crossed through it to the bus and boarded, instantly disappearing, though Jack kept peering through the wet plate-glass window, paying no attention to the young couple in their twenties near him, kissing farewell. The young man said a quick final word to the girl, then turned and hurried out to the bus. The girl stood beside Jack, watching, as the young man followed Buddy up into the bus, and the bus door closed.

For a long second nothing happened.

20

The bus groaned away, as though movement was something alien to it. Jack stood where he was, but the girl moved sideways along the window, paralleling the bus, until she bumped into Jack, startling them both. "Oh!" she cried. "I'm sorry!"

The bus moved on. Jack looked at the girl, saw she was pretty. He grinned at her. "That's okay, I enjoyed it."

The girl seemed drawn to him, seemed about to respond in kind, then remembered herself. She looked past him at the receding bus, then more neutrally again at Jack, saying, "Well. Bye."

"We must do it again sometime," Jack told her.

No response at all. She left the depot and hurried through the rain across the parking lot toward one of the cars waiting there. Jack watched her until his view was cut off by the abrupt appearance of the next bus, its bulk filling the space in front of the window, the sign beside its door reading NEW YORK. Then he blinked, shook his head as though waking up or rousing from hypnosis, and turned to find his luggage: a round, soft bag and a soft suit-carrier. He picked them up.

One door closed. Another opened.

He was smiling by the time he boarded the bus.

And now I'm cold. Why *now*? Why *cold*? It's warm here in the sun, on the slates, on my own land, in my one life, where only the warm is permitted.

It was cold then, that day, the bus station, the girl that crossed my scanners just as the big ship was banking away toward the depths, cold and wet, but I knew nothing of cold then, felt nothing that was cold in those days. Here, now, in my estancia, I feel myself feeling cold despite the warmth here, *señor*, the *muy caliente*. (Is that right? We all learn servant Spanish here, Spiclish, but it can't be trusted; it's at the level of collies barking at sheep, moving the slow and docile creatures through the fences.) *Muy caliente*. But I'm *cold*!

I see that girl's eyes more clearly now than on the day she looked at me in the rain, in the bus depot, when her boyfriend and my friend had gone away, and she was about to turn and walk through the rain to her car. I could have walked with her that day, I could have gone home with her, I could have lain with her on the softly crumpled sheets, our torsos hot, cool flutters on the flesh of our arms, on the backs of our legs, the rain soft on the glass, her eyes looking at me with trust and knowingness. We could have spent forty-seven years in the task, just the two of us, recapturing that first afternoon, or at least reaching for it. Isn't that what marriage is?

But how could I? What choice did I have? I was never free to choose.

Slowly, pulling the robe closed more tightly around my throat, I look at the gray slates and I say, "Sometimes I wonder who I would have been, if I'd just stayed there, you know? In Grover's Corners. Got a job at the bank, got a suit, got married."

The interviewer doesn't speak. The flimsy high clouds write words in an undiscovered alphabet. I'm interviewing myself, I'm doing this clod's work for him. But I don't mind, it's as easy as sleep, it's calm. I'm calm. I can be a very calm person.

"If I'd lived a normal life," I say.

"But you went to New York." The interviewer's voice is neutral, but I know he's interested. Who the fuck is *he*, that he should not be interested?

"New York," I say, and with the words I can see it as it was when I first saw it; jazzy, fast, *full*. And me walking through it, *striding* through it, carrying that round soft bag and that soft suit-carrier. "I loved it, man," I say, and I can hear that sound in my voice. I'm saying *love* as I never said it about any woman, and I know I'm not really saying it about the city but about myself; who I was then, who I planned to be. But I say it again, because this is the surface of the prism we show in the interviews: "I loved that city, everything about it."

"And the acting class?"

"I dropped that fruit right away. I met people, I got taken on by Venashka. Do you know who Venashka was?"

"Famous acting teacher."

"Brilliant," I say, meaning it as a correction. He wasn't a *famous acting teacher*, Venashka, he was *brilliant*. "Brilliant mind," I say, while the sky writes those words in its own language. "Brilliant soul," I say.

"He helped you."

"I learned so *much*. Venashka was such a dynamite person, man, he'd take you right out of yourself. I learned to *be*, you know? Not *act*; any door-to-door salesman can act. To *be*. And I met wonderful people in those classes."

I smile. I'm remembering a girl named Tricia, first girl I ever actually lived with. We were all in the class, on the floor, being dogs. Venashka moved among us, touching a shoulder here, a head there, murmuring encouragement or corrections. I was being a very specific puppy, searching myself for fleas because I wanted to play with them. Venashka moved by, nodding at me, and then I saw Tricia across the way being a hunting dog, pointing at quail. My puppy loped over and sniffed her crotch. She broke character for just a second, shocked, I think maybe even repulsed, and my puppy lolled his tongue and panted at her, bright-eyed. I didn't have a tail, of course, but I wagged it, and I think anybody looking at me would know I was wagging my tail. And Tricia got back into character and reared around to bite me on the shoulder, and that weekend I moved in with her.

The interviewer walks on the garden of my reverie, all unknowing: "Were you just taking classes then? Not acting professionally yet?"

"God, no!" Happy memories bounce me around on the slate like a beach ball. "Making the rounds, trying out for parts. Trying to be a real *actor*! Incredible!"

FLASHBACK 4

The theater was small, with black walls and only simple efficient lighting on the stage. Twenty James Deans lurked and posed and fixed their hair in the main auditorium, while another James Dean, script in hand, went through a scene on stage, playing opposite Miriam Croft, a famous older actress, a one-time beauty who was now most frequently called "well preserved." Miss Croft, working without a script, her manner imperious and demanding, said, "'I *am* your mother, and I *do* love you.'"

"'You don't love me,'" the James Dean read, passionately. "'You *never* loved me. You never loved *anybody*. You don't know *how* to love.'"

"All right," called the director from the front row. A tall, thin man with a thick black mustache and waving hands, he was known for his impatience. Of the half-dozen people watching from the front row, he was the only one without notepad or clipboard. "Thank you very much," he said to the James Dean on stage. "Next."

The James Dean shrugged and walked off into the wings

and Jack entered smiling like someone who wants to be helpful. Jack carried no script. While Miriam Croft watched him, noncommittal, he stepped to the center of the stage and faced front.

An assistant, seated to the left of the director, clutched her clipboard and pen and called, "Name?"

"Jack Pine."

"Do we have your résumé?"

Easy, confident, self-deprecating, Jack spread his hands and said, "Such as it is."

The director, edginess in his voice, said, "Where's your script?"

"Oh, I've been hearing the scene," Jack told him. "I know it now."

The director shook his head, waved his hand. "Then go right ahead."

Jack turned to look at Miriam Croft, and at once he altered, he transmogrified, he became someone else. He was taller and thinner, both more closed off and yet more vulnerable. He was cold, mistrustful, in pain. Miriam cocked an eyebrow, watching him.

Jack's voice seemed nearly closed, half strangling him, when at last he spoke: "'Mother . . .'"

Irritably, the director called, "The line is, 'Mother, I can't stay.'"

Miriam, quite serious, watching Jack unblinking, said, "He knows the line, Harry."

The director reared back. "Well, excuse me."

Amiable, helpful, his former self, Jack smiled pleasantly at the director, saying, "Are we ready now, sir?"

Miffed but professional, the director said, "Of course. Go right ahead."

"Thank you, sir," Jack said, and turned back to Miriam, and again underwent that transition to the other person, the unhappy defeated son: "'Mother . . . I can't stay.'"

"'But I insist, darling.'"

Jack turned, twisted, a caged animal searching for a nonexistent door. "'You . . . stifle me. There's no *air* in here, I can't breathe.'"

Miriam's eyes were fastened like cargo hooks on Jack's face. "'I only want what's best for you, dear. I am your mother, and I do love you.'"

The words were wrung from Jack, blasphemies he was helpless not to pronounce: "'You don't love me. You *never* loved me. You never loved *anybody*. You don't know *how* to love.'"

Miriam smiled.

I smile. The sun slides free, looks down on me. The sun, methinks, looks with a watery eye. But which of us was Titania, which was Bottom?

The interviewer says, "That was your first professional role."

"True. True."

"And Miriam Croft was a great help to you."

"We were a great help to one another," I say, and I laugh. But it hurts to laugh. I seem to be nothing but broken ribs from neck to crotch when I laugh, so I stop laughing. I smile. "We helped one another in so many ways," I say.

FLASHBACK 5

At night, the view from Miriam Croft's bedroom window was of a magnificent swath of dark, twenty-seven stories below, pinked with warm and creamy lights; the stretch of Central Park extending from in front of her building on West 59th Street two and a half miles north to 110th Street, flanked by the bright towers and armed fortresses of Manhattan. The George Washington Bridge was a jeweled necklace in the far upper left of the view, a number of neoned corporate logos made glittering brooches at the throats of nearer buildings, and now and then a slow-moving hansom cab became briefly visible as it passed through the illumination of a park light far below, hinting at a gentler and more romantic age.

A magnificent view, but at this moment Miriam Croft was not observing it. At this moment, Miriam, her contact lenses out, was blurrily observing her bedroom ceiling, while Jack, atop her, performed like mad. "Oh, my Gaaaaa-*aahhhhd!*" Miriam cried out, and Jack raced to catch up, and they crossed the finish line together, spent, panting, their two hearts pounding as one. "Oh," Miriam said, her arms gripping him tightly around the back. "Oh. Oh."

"Mmm, Miriam," he murmured, smiling against her perfumed but crapen neck. Gradually he permitted more and more of his weight to rest on her, until she would want him off; at last she did, releasing him, sighing with long contentment, sliding her long-fingered hands from his back.

Then he lifted himself, rearing up on extended arms, beaming down at her, delighted in them both. "Well, well, Miriam!" he cried. "You *are* all right!"

Irony, briefly lost, had returned to Miriam. Stroking his cheek, smiling, she said, "The workman is as good as his tool, dear."

"You can teach me so *much*!" Jack cried.

Miriam's smile turned acid, became cold amusement. "And the first lesson, dear," she said, "is don't be too eager."

"But I *am* eager, Miriam," Jack cried, laughing at the truth of it. "I'm eager for everything, I'm eager to be, to be *used*!" Rolling off her, sitting up tailor-fashion, resting one hand on her lowest rib, he said, "I am a good actor, aren't I?"

She nodded, slowly, solemnly, treating it as a serious question. "Probably better than you know," she said. "And you aren't even afraid of it, are you?"

"Why should I be?" he asked, astonished. "It makes me happy!"

"And you are going to make me happy," she told him. "And there are no dangers at all in the world."

"Not in our world," he said.

Mow the years collide! And here I am, after all, while the past bounces and rattles away like tools left in the trunk of a car. How can I describe this to my friendly neighborhood interviewer? I cannot. I will not. These are *my* memories. "Ah, Miriam," I say.

"Miriam Croft," the interviewer says, and I can hear him imperfectly hide his disapproval. But who asked for his approval? He says, "She must have been forty years older than you."

"Forty-three, in fact," I say, amused after all this time by that strange fact. Doubly amused by the interviewer with his narrow little views.

"You had an affair with her," says this prissy little man.

Disapproval gives me strength. All at once, it is possible for me to rise to a seated position, legs folded on the slate. I tuck the robe down between my legs—no use offending him that way as well—and I say, "She *kept* me, pal. That was an off-Broadway show we were doing. Her name wasn't that big anymore, and the pay was peanuts. But

31

Miriam got me the job and moved me into her Central Park South apartment. She bought me my first really good wardrobe, she introduced me to people, and she taught me how to not be too eager. Miriam was very good for me, and I think I was pretty good for her, too. Brightened her last days, you might say."

Amusement makes me weak. I recline again, slowly, not wanting to crack the old beano on the slate. Very valuable slate, you know. I lie down. I smile at the sky. The interviewer waits, so I say it: "Brightened her last moments, in point of fact."

FLASHBACK 6

The limousine rolling north-eastward through the dusk on the New England Thruway, that strip of high-speed road between New York City and the Connecticut state line, was a gleaming tasteful black, with New York plates indicating it had been either leased or rented. The chauffeur was a serious-looking white man of close to sixty, in a black suit, white shirt, narrow black tie, and black uniform cap. The glass partition between him and the spacious rear compartment of the limousine was closed, and from the point of view of the front seat the rear seemed to be empty.

It was nearly eight in the evening of a midweek day in spring. The air outside was soft, the sky pearlescent, the traffic not at all bad, considering the realities of the BosWash Corridor. The driver was accomplished, the limousine in excellent condition, the voyage smooth and tension-free.

A sign passed on the right. The driver, noting it, lifted the telephone from near his right knee on the dashboard and spoke into it: "We are entering Connecticut, madam."

Immediately, Jack's head rose into view on the other side of the partition. He was laughing, his eyes manic. He gazed in the rearview mirror at the reflection of the driver's face—the driver's eyes remained fixed on the road ahead—then groped for the rear seat telephone and spoke into it.

The metallic voice sounded in the driver's ear: "And that ain't all we're entering, James. We'll need fifteen minutes."

Not a flicker of expression touched the driver's face. Correct, unflappable, he said, "Yes, sir."

Jack, laughing, extended the phone down out of sight toward the floor in back. More faintly, his metallic voice sounded from the phone the driver held to his ear: "Do you wish to speak to James, madam?"

Another voice sounded, equally metallic, but identifiable as that of Miriam Croft. At first she was merely laughing, but then she said, "Halliwell, just keep driving, dear, until we tell you otherwise."

"Yes, madam."

Less distinct, too far from the phone, Jack said, "How about me, madam? Should *I* keep driving?"

Miriam's laughter was loud, then farther away, as Jack took the phone from her and spoke into it again, grinning through the glass at the driver "We'll just keep driving, James, you and me, right *through* Connecticut! Can we do that?"

Miriam's laughter sputtered and struggled as she fought for breath, trying to talk and laugh and inhale all at once, crying out, "Oh, no! Oh, don't! Oh, poor Halliwell!" but then the laughter broke into pieces, into choking and gasping, into wheezing and terrible retching sounds.

Jack stared downward, suddenly concerned, then frightened, the phone in his hand obviously forgotten. Through it, the driver heard him cry, "Miriam? Miriam! Jesus *God*, put your tongue in! Miriam! Not you, too!"

Dropping the phone, Jack poked and prodded at the out-of-sight Miriam, while the chokes and gasps weakened. Then he turned to the driver, panicky, pounding on the glass, yelling, his words barely audible at all until he remembered the phone and dived for it. The driver, unsure what was going on and knowing that practical jokes were not impossible with these people, at last frowned at the rearview mirror, in which the wild-eyed and terrified Jack suddenly reappeared, phone mashed to his ear as he yelled, "Help! She's having a fit or something! Find a hospital!"

This was no practical joke. "Yes, *sir!*" answered the driver, and pressed the accelerator to the floor.

And so the limousine tore through the sweet-scented Connecticut night, trailing Jack's screams, Jack's moans, Jack's brokenhearted cry: "Miriam! *Please!* Pull yourself together!" And across the empty lanes his final, fatal scream: "Not *agaaiiinnn!*"

There are things I shall not
tell this interviewer. Wild torsos could not drag them out
of me, though they're invited to try.

On the other hand—is it the other hand, or another part
of the same hand? A different finger?—on the other finger,
then, there are things I shall not even tell *myself*. In fact, so
clever am I, perched atop this other finger, that I shall not
even tell myself what the things are that I shall not tell
myself. And to think people say drugs affect the brain; not
my brain, Pops.

Between the things I shall not tell myself and the things
I shall not tell the interviewer are those incidents, those
memories that can still cause pain but not to an unbear-
able degree. Such as, to take the example that slots neatly
into its chronological space at this juncture, the funeral of
Miriam. Facing the patient silent interviewer with my
blandest and most untroubled smile, I relive that troubled
time.

A lot of people blamed me for what happened to Miriam,
but my doctors said it wasn't my fault. She'd already had

two minor strokes, which she hadn't told anybody (including me) about, and it could have happened at any time. And, as far as I was concerned, Miriam had checked out just exactly the way she would have wanted, coming and going at the same glorious moment. But you couldn't explain that to a lot of thin-lipped nieces and nephews.

Miriam had found me an agent—her own, of course, Jack Schullmann—and Jack phoned to say if I went to the funeral he'd drop me as a client and do his best to blackball me in the theater. He was an important man in that bitchy world, but I told him to go fuck himself. If he and the rest of them wanted to take away everything that Miriam had given me, that was all right, too. Bury me with her like an Egyptian servant, I didn't care.

So I did go to the funeral, and a hard-eyed usher made me sit in the back row. No one spoke to me or acknowledged my presence in any way, but that was the first time my picture ran in the *National Enquirer*. Is that funny, or what?

Jack Schullmann was as good as his word; after Miriam's funeral, when I finally came out again, I too was dead. But *really* dead. I made the rounds the same as ever, hit the auditions, sent my résumé to every other agent in town (none of them wanted me, not then), but nothing happened, and in truth my heart just wasn't in it. But then one night . . .

But this is something I can report aloud, a spot where I can bring the interviewer aboard again, give him a little whadayacallit—*frisson*. That's it. Got a *frisson* for you, pal. "After Miriam's death," I begin, but then I cloud over briefly, and when my internal sky once more is clear the interviewer is still there, politely waiting, pen poised, eyebrows lifted in respectful attention. "Yes," I say. "After . . . that, I was lost for a while. I didn't know where to go, what to do, who I should try to be. I still had my friends from the classes and all that, we still all hung out together, went to parties, but I felt distant, not really a part of the scene. I knew that no matter how it might look from outside, I didn't care for anybody else, and

37

nobody else cared for me. And without the acting, without *using* myself, with nobody to be but me, I was empty, I was nothing. I guess that's about as alone as I ever got."

The interviewer nods, viewing me with faint (possibly professional) sympathy. "How long did that go on?" he asks. "That sense of . . . separateness?"

"Separateness?" I laugh, hurting my throat. *"That's* permanent," I say. "But the trouble after Miriam died? Almost a year, all in all. Until the following summer, when one night at a party I ran into Harry Robelieu, the director of the play where I'd met Miriam, and he asked me what I was doing that weekend, was I free or what, there was somebody he wanted me to meet. So I told him I was free, and God knows that was true, and that was how I first went to Fire Island Pines and met George Castleberry."

FLASHBACK 7

The far blue sea was full to the brim, rolling up the white sand lip of shore and receding again, flowing and ebbing, frothing white, whispering to itself while up on the silver-bleached wooden deck the pretty people in white trousers and powerful people in multicolored muumuus chattered together amid a jingling music of ice cubes. The deck served as collar for an oval swimming pool in which two bronzed young men in bikini briefs played and giggled, their fingers from time to time brushing as though inadvertently each other's thighs. The bikinis bulged, the eyes sparkled like the sea, the pink tongues lolled in their mouths.

Beyond the pool and deck was the house, all white and glass, broadside to the sea, extending to the right beyond the deck. Through open sliding glass doors was the wide main room, at once parlor, dining area, and kitchen. In here, among the white walls, blond furniture, and large semierotic paintings, more people, all of them male (like those outside), chatted and drank and ate the delicate canapés. The kitchen was at the right end, and beyond it stretched a skylit hall flanked by doors—master bedroom and bath on the ocean side, guest rooms and bath on the poison ivy side—with an open door at the far end leading to a room enclosed by crowded bookshelves, with small windows grudging an ocean view and a desk against the windowless farthest wall. In this room, hunched over a small portable typewriter on the desk, sat the owner of the house, George Castleberry, trying to get some work done.

It was always the same thing every summer. Get into a social mood, invite friends, accept friends of friends because the whole world and his gay brother wants to come to Fire Island Pines, and when the house fills up discover there's just too much work to be done, deadlines are pressing, the whole thing was just a dreadful mistake. The typewriter calls, duty calls, let the damn locusts amuse themselves, they'll all be gone on the last ferry anyway, *no* sleepovers. Except, of course, for those very few, that tiny number, that infinitesimal troop of those George Castleberry actually *liked*. Then he could settle down with that hardy band for the true amusement of the day: dishing the day trippers.

In the meantime, work. It was so hard to *concentrate*; while his guests cavorted, George frowned furiously at the leaden words he had most recently typed. A slender petulant balding man of fifty-three, dressed in a green and white caftan and brown sandals, George Castleberry was among the three or four most powerful playwrights of the current American stage, and yet it seemed to him when working that every word he put on paper was meretricious and false, that he had been incredibly lucky in the matter of actors and directors and producers, that he was a fraud and a mountebank who would inevitably some day be exposed for the utter waste of everybody's time he really was, that it was only the deplorable state of the American theater—all the really *talented* writers were either doing novels for the art or movies for the money—that had made it possible for him to get away with this fourth-rate toothless mumbling for as long as he had. Having to fight his way past *that* clawing gorgon in his mind to the typewriter every day left him not much time or patience for the sensibilities of others. Now, hearing light laughter more distinctly than the general background wash of social chitchat, he snarled, he actually *ground his teeth*, he turned to glare over his shoulder and down the long hall to where some pretty pansy all in white stood twinkling in amusement, just beyond the threshold into the kitchen. "Damnit!" George cried. "Close that door!"

Startled faces were turned toward him. Two or three people reached at once for the knob, bumping into one another, creating a brief Keystone Komedy before at last the door was shut and he was alone.

Still angry, George turned to the typewriter and glared at the words written there. "Now I don't get the ventilation," he muttered, anger shading into self-pity.

Two or three minutes of despairing concentration quite slowly elapsed. George's fingers moved tentatively to the typewriter keys, tapped out a word, another, another, a phrase, a sentence, another.

A breeze riffled the page in the typewriter. Party chat became audible again. George, one eyebrow raised in murderous disbelief, turned about to see Harry Robelieu making his way down the hall toward this room, diffident but daring. Robelicu, a minor director of off-Broadway or out-of-town productions, was among those tolerated by but not actually welcomed by George; his brazen approach now, no matter how tremulous, was so unexpected that George said nothing, didn't even snarl, scarcely showed his teeth as Harry traversed the hall and entered the office and said, "George, we just came over on the ferry."

Deceptively quiet, George said, "I'm *trying* to *work* here."

Harry, unbelievably, didn't even acknowledge that. Some sort of excitement gleamed beneath his pale anonymous face. He said, "There's someone I want you to meet."

"I don't want to meet people," George told him. "I hate people. What have people ever done for me?"

"This isn't people," Harry insisted, moving toward the sea-view window. "Come take a look."

George sat where he was. Harry looked out the window, then back at George, gesturing to him to come see. George turned his head to glower at his typewriter, needing to struggle through to victory, but at the same time tempted by this distraction, intrigued despite himself by Harry's unwonted manner. With an angry slap of the hand on the desktop, he rose and crossed toward the window, prepared to be coldly bitchy about anything at all Harry might have it in mind to show. "Yes?" he said.

"Look," Harry said, gesturing again, stepping back from the window.

George looked, lips already curling.

All alone by himself, at the outer corner of the silver-gray deck, stood a magnificent boy of twenty-three or -four, in tight black T-shirt and white jeans. He was half turned away, one hand on hip, gazing out over the illimitable sea. Sunlight caressed the strong line of his jaw, shadowed the eyes beneath his brows.

"Marc Antony," whispered George.

"His name's Jack Pine," Harry Robelieu said, smiling with mingled amusement and relief. "If you want, I'll—"

George turned, ignoring the soft, stupid man, and crossed the room with suddenly certain strides. Down the hall he went, and diagonally through the long main room to the open glass doors. Surprised and happy voices spoke to him, mistakenly assuming he had finished his work for the day, but he brushed uncaring by their faces, glasses, smiles, babbling words, gestures of comradeship and welcome.

Outside, the sun was very bright, almost a physical presence through which he marched, around the pool and across the deck, as though he and the boy were alone on a platform on a high mountaintop somewhere, the highest mountain in the world. A breeze whipped the caftan around his legs as he strode, the giggling and splashing from the pool faded to vacuity, and George stood before the boy.

Slowly, Jack Pine's sea-struck eyes drew in, darkened, refocused down from the far horizon. George smiled at him. The boy, uncertain, tried an answering smile, saying, "Hello?"

George took the boy's hands in both his own. "Do you know?" he said, his voice melting, all his pain and doubt draining away, leaving him as light as air. "Do you know? I've just written an entire play all about you, and here we are, meeting for the very first time."

How beautiful the ocean was that day. I've always been very interested in water. (Not today, though; today I have no interest in looking at that pool of mine, just over there somewhere beyond the gray slate patio. I seem to be sitting up again, bent slightly forward for balance, terry-cloth robe fallen from my knuckly knees and bunched before my crotch. I seem to be half-turned away from that charming pool of mine, my face seems to be very near the polite but businesslike and very properly clad knee of my interviewer, who gazes down past that knee of his at me with what I now perceive to be horror and shock. What on earth have I been telling him? Oh, gosh, yes, George. Old George. I chuckle.)

The chuckle goads a reaction from my friend with the pad. Repugnance half strangling his voice, he says, "You went to *bed* with George Castleberry?"

"Waterbed," I say, explain, explicate further, and the memory of that oceanic encounter, full of slipperinesses and heaving and absurd near misses makes me chuckle again.

44

The interviewer is appalled, well and truly appalled. "But—" he says, stutters, stumbles, "but—you're completely heterosexual! All those marriages, all those girlfriends, all those children!"

I shrug, nod, acquiesce, explain: "It was a great part."

"A great *part*!"

"I wanted it," I say. "I am an actor, that's what I *am*. When I don't work, when I can't work, I get into all these *things*, all this trouble. After Miriam, after Jack Schullmann blackballed me in the theater, after the empty months of being nothing and nobody and having no idea where I was going or if I was going *anywhere*, I wanted it. The role of Biff Novak was the only thing in the world at that particular moment that I really and truly wanted. So I got it. And the emptiness went away."

"You had *sex* with George Castleberry!" Has ever an interviewer before in history had such large, round eyes?

"Mostly," I say, "George had sex with me."

Those large, round eyes blink, the mouth purses. "I'm not sure how that works," he says.

I reach up a hand, mildly surprised at how badly it's shaking, and tug at his nearest trouser knee. "It's easy to understand," I say. "Take off your pants."

Nervously, betraying his nervousness, he taps my knuckles with his pencil to make me stop tugging at him. "That's not necessary, Mr. Pine," he says.

I remove my hand from him. This hand is *really* shaking. "The necessary we do right now," I say, watching the hand. "The incoherent takes a little longer." Turning my head a bit, bracing myself with a palm against the cool slate so I don't inadvertently knock myself over with the force of my projection, "Hoskins!" I shout.

"The point is," the prissy interviewer says, viewing me with loathing, "the point is, you slept your way to the top."

"I did not." I frown at him in offended dignity. "I slept my way to the middle," I correct him frostily. "I *clawed* my way to the top."

"However it happened," he says, still coldly upset with

me, "you did get the part of Biff Novak, the lead, in *Last Seen in Tupelo*."

This is a statement, not a question. Having nothing to answer, I once again turn my head and raise my voice: "Hoskins, dammit!"

Immediately he appears, as though dropped from an airplane. He is my butler, and by God he *looks* it. White-haired, stoutish without being obese, stone-faced, dressed in full fig, he is as much a symbol of my status as my Mercedes. Bowing correctly from the hips, he speaks with that proper English-butler accent of his (I love it!): "You called?"

"I bellowed, dammit," I tell him. "That's your line, Hoskins, as you well know." Imitating him perfectly, a thing I'm good at, and dipping my head in pale shadow of his obeisance, I say, "You bellowed, sir?"

Imitating me perfectly, not a flicker of expression on his patrician face as he dips his head in pale shadow of true obeisance, he says, "You bellowed, sir?'"

"I did." I show Hoskins my shaking hand. For some reason, I'm not sure why, I believe him to be sympathetic behind that blank facade. "I want one of those fuzzy drink things, you know?" I say. "With the vodka and the milk and the egg and all that stuff."

"Certainly, sir," he says (what else would he say?), and turns to the interviewer. "Anything for you, sir?"

The interviewer seems embarrassed as well as sur-prised. With a fidgety laugh, he indicates his notepad and pencil. "Not on duty," he says.

Strange thing to say.

Hoskins doesn't think so. "Very well," he says, and bows generally and exits.

Where am I? Something's gone agley with this inter-view, this fella dislikes me now. That's not the way it's done; we get *along* with the press. Trying for a cheery smile, I say, "Very restoring, that drink thing. Gets me on my feet. Knees, anyway. Where were we?"

"*Last Seen in Tupelo*." He still disapproves of me; damn his eyes.

"Right," I say. "That play made me, of course. Biff Novak was the real start of it all." Smiling in reminiscence, I say, "And it brought Buddy back into my life."

"Your best friend."

"That's right." I smile, seeing it as a camera shot. AN ANGLE on a theater marquee:

Saul Katz Presents
GEORGE CASTLEBERRY'S
L A S T S E E N I N T U P E L O
starring

JACK PINE   MARCIA CALLAHAN

CAMERA PANS down from the marquee to a busy midtown New York street, centering on Buddy Pal, standing on the sidewalk in marine uniform and close-cropped hair, duffel bag over shoulder, smiling up at the marquee.

"Buddy Pal," I say.

FLASHBACK 8

The dressing room was windowless and small but elegantly and expensively appointed. The style might have been just a bit *too* masculine, protesting just that shade too much in its elkhorn ashtray and brown leather sofa with discreet brass nailheads around its bottom and the Remington reproduction (cavalry charge) on the wall. When the makeup lights flanking the mirrored dressing table were off, as now, the indirect lighting made the room softly mellow and cozy, like some underwater grotto where Captain Nemo might relax, the rich browns and creams a pleasant relief from that infernal eternal blue.

Seated on the sofa, in passionate but still-clothed embrace, were the two stars of the show, Jack Pine and Marcia Callahan, she a forthright brunette of twenty-eight, tall and slender, whose seventh starring role in a Broadway show—and seventh affair with her leading man—this was. Or would be. Or might be.

Jack found himself kissing Marcia's eyebrow, and then her forehead, and then the top of her head, realizing her lips and hands were working their way down the front of his body, destination unmistakable. With a little surprised smile, the visual equivalent of *Jeepers!* he shifted to a position more comfortable for them both, relaxed, smiled more lazily, then all at once sat up again, pulling up the bewildered woman by the shoulders, saying, "Marcia, no. Better not."

She gazed at him with bewilderment in her forthright eyes. "Are you kidding?"

Embarrassed, his less-than-forthright gaze slipping away from her, he mumbled, "George."

"George?"

"He's due here any minute," Jack said, unhappy but trapped. "He'll want me to be pleased to see him, if you know what I mean."

"Oh." Understanding made her back away along the sofa, adjusting her clothing. Glancing down at him with dismissive scorn, she said, "That's right. I was forgetting where it's been."

They both got to their feet, as a knock sounded at the door and a voice called, "Ten minutes to curtain. Ten minutes to curtain."

"I heard you, I heard you," Jack snapped at the closed door. Turning to Marcia, he said, "George made this whole thing possible for me. I owe him . . . I owe him everything, Marcia. There'll be time for us."

"I think maybe our time is all used up," Marcia said.

"Don't say that. You know how I feel about—"

Another knock sounded at the door. "I *heard* you!"

Marcia laughed, lightly. The doorknob rattled. Marcia said, "It isn't the warning, it's your playmate. See you on stage, lover."

She opened the door, fixing her face into the false smile to be presented to the author of the play, but it was Buddy who entered instead, in his uniform and carrying his duffel bag over his shoulder, saying happily to Marcia, "Well, look at you, will you."

"My mistake," Marcia said. "The *rough* trade is here."

Easy and amused with her, Buddy said, "Don't be misled, doll. I can be very gentle."

"Buddy!" Jack cried. "You're here!"

"Sure I am," Buddy said. "How you doin', Dad?"

Jack embraced his friend, holding tight. Buddy returned the embrace but looked over Jack's shoulder to grin at Marcia, who watched with some uncertainty, not exactly sure what was going on here.

It was Buddy who ended the clinch at last, saying, "Let me breathe, Dad."

"Oh, sure, Buddy, sure!" Turning to Marcia, grinning in delight, holding Buddy's elbow, Jack said, "Marcia, this is my oldest friend in the whole world, Buddy Pal. We grew up together."

"That's nice," Marcia said.

"Buddy," Jack said, pride and pleasure in his every atom, "this is Marcia Callahan, my co-star in the show."

"I recognized her from the pictures out front," Buddy said. Grinning at Marcia, looking her up and down, he said, "In person, you don't have too much on top, do you?"

"On top of what?" Marcia asked him.

They'd left the dressing room door open, and now George Castleberry appeared in the doorway, melting face in a loving smile at first, but then becoming immediately irritable as he looked around the room. "Well," he said. "A crowd."

"I'm just going, George," Marcia said.

But George's mood had changed again; he gazed with amused pleasure on Buddy in his marine uniform, saying, "Be still, my heart. Is that *real*?"

"Sure is," Buddy told him. "Just got out of the marines two days ago. Don't have my civvies yet."

"Well, never change, that's my advice," George told him.

Turning to Jack, Buddy said, "In fact, Dad, that's why I came by. If you could tide me over . . ."

"Oh, sure, Buddy," Jack said, his smile suddenly nervous, uneasy. "How much do you need?"

"A hundred or so."

"No problem, Buddy," Jack said. Taking his wallet from

his hip pocket, his movements and expressions awkward and clumsy, he made introductions while counting money into Buddy's waiting palm: "George Castleberry, our playwright, I'd like you to meet my old friend Buddy Pal."

Dryly, Marcia said, "They grew each other up together."

"Doll, it's you for me," Buddy told her. Linking his arm with hers, he said, "Would you like to see my old war wound?"

Amused by him, intrigued by him, she permitted him to lead her from the room, saying as she went, "I don't know. Would I?"

George closed the door after them, then turned to Jack with arms outstretched. "Dear boy," he said.

Jack performed a boyish smile. "Hi, George."

A knock sounded at the door, and a voice called, "Five minutes to curtain. Five minutes to curtain."

Jack took George's hands, held them in his, a movement that seemed to suggest togetherness but which nevertheless subtly kept George at a little distance. "I'm sorry, George," Jack said. "It's too late."

Petulant, George said, "Traffic was *terrible*. I hate this city, I really do."

Jack did truly like his benefactor, and his sympathy showed through his nervousness and reluctance. "I'm sorry," he said again. "I have to go."

"Later," George told him. "I'll see you here later. After the performance."

His smile wan, Jack said, "After the performance, the performance."

George leaned forward to kiss Jack's cheek. Jack awkwardly patted the older man's back, then moved gracefully around him and left the room, closing the door behind himself.

George roved the tiny room, wringing his hands, a series of agonized expressions on his face, small moaning sounds rising from his throat. At last he flung himself into the chair in front of the dressing table and stared desperately at his own reflection. "You *fool*, you," he cried, and put his head down onto his folded arms and wept.

51

How it all comes back to me now, those wonderful days of first success, when I was still young and naive and hopeful and *caring*. I had such genius in those days! I could do anything. And with Buddy again at my side . . . Buddy would always save me, protect me, keep me from harm. He'd been doing it from the beginning. (We don't—we *never*—talk about that.)

I sit smiling at the patio, under God's sun (the high clouds have cleared away, but I'm not even afraid of *that* anymore), and I bask in my memories of those glorious days, until I notice the interviewer frowning at me again. *Now* what's his problem? "Something wrong?" I ask.

He says, "Wait a minute. That last part. Where George Castleberry looked at himself in the mirror and said, 'You fool, you,' and put his head down on his folded arms and wept."

I nod, agreeing. "A lovely scene, isn't it? Touching, dramatic, full of pathos and understanding and deep revelation."

"But," he says, "you didn't see that part. That happened after you left the room."

"One knows these things," I say, and Hoskins rolls into view like a giant passenger ship, possibly the *QEII*, bearing a tall, shimmering glass on a silver tray. "Ah, Hoskins," I say.

"Your fuzzy drink, sir."

"Thank you, Hoskins."

Hoskins recedes, like one of those literary ghosts—Scrooge's father, Hamlet's Christmas—and I raise the shimmering glass. "To Marcia Callahan," I say.

"Your first wife, I believe," the interviewer says. They love to show how they've *researched* you, how they've *studied up* on you, how they've *done their homework*. There are times when I hate being other people's homework.

I taste the shimmer in the glass, and it is like all the finest things of our planet gathered together into one foamy tube. The clean chill of Antarctica, the breezy pure sweetness of the Caribbean, the tang of giant cities everywhere. Oh, my goodness me!

"Marcia Callahan," I say, and pause to lick ambrosia from my upper lip. "I guess you could call it love-hate at first sight. We never had any illusions about each other, Marcia and me, but maybe that was why we were so drawn together. We were naked for each other. *I* was certainly naked for *her*."

I smile, thinking back, reliving again our most famous scene from the play: Marcia, in various shawls and laces, sits on a park bench. I, in T-shirt and jeans and heavy workboots, roam the stage, circling her, ranting and raging. She replies in soft but compelling counterpoint, fighting back with tattered dignity. And night after night, alone in the forwardmost box to stage left, his marine uniform replaced by a gleaming new tux I'd bought him, Buddy Pal sat and watched. In my pacing of the stage, flinging my arms about, roaring, letting it all out, I would sometimes look up and see him there, a faint smile on his face as he watched Marcia. And from time to time, in her self-defense, Marcia would look bravely up past me at that box high on the theater's side wall, where Buddy sat concealed from the rest of the audience by plush drapes. I sigh and smile, and the shimmery glass trembles in my trembling hand.

"After Buddy got out of the marines," I say, "the three of us were inseparable. It was like old times, but even better. We were going to be together forever.'"

"But you weren't," the interviewer says.

"The show closed. They made a movie out of it, and they hired Marcia to what they call re-create the role. But they didn't want me."

"I'm surprised," the interviewer says.

"Are you? Well, you don't know shit about showbiz, do you? No," I say quickly, "forget that, sorry, that was just this drink talking, nice fuzzy drink."

"I imagine," he says, gently, forgiving me, "I imagine the memory of that can still hurt."

"Most memories still hurt," I say, and laugh, and catch myself before I spill this *wonderful* fuzzy drink. "The thing is," I say, "they had some guy under contract, some guy they were *grooming*. Marcia was already a star, and I was just some guy that was in her last play. So they put in this fucking twerp they were *grooming*. Eventually, the critics told them they were crazy, but by then it was too late."

The interviewer nods. I have his sympathy back, all right; there's nothing they hate more than success, and nothing they love more than failure. Feed them great fat shovelfuls of humility and abasement and defeat, and they'll feed *you* more and more success. Love it!

He says, with his new sympathetic voice, "What did you do then?"

"Nothing," I say. "Marcia moved out to the Coast, of course, to make the movie. George and I broke up as soon as the play closed—funny thing, it was as much his doing as mine—and Buddy and I went on living together in a little place I had on East 18th Street."

Wide-eyed, about to call back his sympathy vote, my interviewer said, "You were having an affair with *Buddy Pal?*"

I stare at him, truly shocked and outraged. "Are you

crazy? I'm not that way! Buddy isn't—for God's sake, man, we're both straight!"

Confused, abashed, the interviewer leans back in his chair, nodding agreement with me, saying, "Sorry, sorry, I just got a little confused there, you know, after George Castleberry and all that kind of—"

"That, fella," I say, "is what we in the biz call a career move. It has nothing to do with the inner man, you see what I mean?"

"It's cynical, you mean," he says.

I beam at him. Dear fuzzy drink, fuzzing around through all my suburbs, turning me on like neons at nighttime. "My friend," I say, "you just used a word that has no meaning."

His face is blank. "I did?"

"*Cynical.* You see, my friend, it's a spectrum," I say, and spread my hands like a fisherman lying, and very nearly, very nearly, very damn *nearly* spill the remains of my fuzzy drink, but recover in time and continue: "It's a spectrum," I say. "Here at this end is the romantic, and over here at this end is the cynic. So wherever you are on this here spectrum here, you're the realist, and everybody on that side is too much of a romantic, and everybody on that side is too much of a cynic."

"Is that right?"

"That's right," I say, seeing no need to disagree with myself. "More examples. You take a normal interest in your job. Everybody on *this* side of you is lazy, and everybody on *that* side of you is a workaholic. Or everybody on one side is frigid, and everybody on the other side's a nymphomaniac. Or everybody over here's—"

"I get the idea," he assures me loudly, interrupting a fine flow, a fine fuzzy-drink-induced flow, and then he hurries on to keep that fine flow from starting up again, asking me, "Did you get another part in a play after *Last Seen in Tupelo* closed?"

"No," I tell him, clouding over slightly, the fuzzy drink beginning to curdle within me at the memory of that empty time in my life, Buddy pressing me to bring in some money, the great lethargy creeping over me, all my troubles and woes, the memories I hadn't learned how to jam. . . . "Jack Schullmann's blackball against me was still alive then," I explain to this button-eyed interviewer, "and during that time I was with George I did more drinking than maybe I should have at such a tender age—not like now! Hah!" And I finish the fuzzy drink!

"So what did you do?" this dull fellow asks me.

I radiate pleasure in his direction. "I got married," I say simply.

FLASHBACK 9

On her way home from the studio, Marcia picked up her dry cleaning, then continued on up and over Beverly Glen Boulevard out of the Valley and into Westwood to the furnished rental she'd taken while shooting *Tupelo*. The house was modified mission-style, one story high, with red tiled roof and beige stucco walls, the structure sprawling over most of the available property, with neat lawn and shrubbery in front and a large swimming pool filling the space in back.

Hooked to the visor of the rented Porsche was the box that controlled the door of the attached garage; Marcia thumbed the button on that box as she made the turn into her driveway, and the broad blank door folded up and back, receding into the open mouth of the garage like a piece of stage magician's equipment. Marcia drove from the sunny exterior to the dark oily-smelling interior of the garage, unnaturally bare and neat inside (this being a short-term rental), and behind her the door slid out and swept down, as though the house had just ingested another victim.

Marcia collected the plastic dry-cleaner bag, which had been draped over the back of the passenger seat, then climbed from the car and went through the connecting door into the kitchen. She passed through the kitchen and out the other side, then moved diagonally across one corner of the long, low living room with its low beige furniture and broad, chrome-faced fireplace. A long hall led from there, with more rooms to the right and a wall of glass on the left overlooking the swimming pool and its redwood surround. Walking down this hall, the dry-cleaner bag held over her shoulder like Frank Sinatra's jacket, Marcia glanced leftward and saw, in profile, Jack Pine.

It was him, all right. In cowboy hat and fringed jacket and high decorated boots, he sat in a very low canvas chair at the deep end of the pool, seated well down and back so his head and knees were at the same height, cowboy hat pulled low over his eyes to shade them from the afternoon sun, booted legs stretched far out in front of him over the redwood deck with ankles crossed, hands folded casually in lap. From a cigarette in the corner of his mouth, a slender pale tendril of smoke wavered upward past his ear and the brim of his hat.

Marcia did not break stride. Her eyes narrowed slightly, she gazed steadily at that self-absorbed profile out there, and she kept walking, on down to the end of the hall, where she faced front again at last, moving through the doorway into the master bedroom.

A battered round, soft traveling bag and an equally well-worn soft suit-carrier lay on the bed. Nodding as though to say her expectations had been fulfilled, she walked around the bed to the wall of closets and hung the dry-cleaning bag on the rod. Then she turned, looked again at the luggage on the bed, took a long, slow breath, and glanced across the room at her reflection in the dressing mirror there. No expression showed in the face looking back at her.

A sliding glass door led from the bedroom to the pool, near its shallow end. Marcia stepped through, slid the door shut behind her, and looked down across the water at Jack, who hadn't moved. An almost inaudible sigh parted her lips, which then pressed shut again. Deliberately she strode around the pool. He finally—as she was halfway to him—lifted his head and lifted his hand to lift his cowboy hat away from his eyes to watch her. Nothing else on him moved.

Marcia stopped in front of him. They looked at each other for a long silent moment, and Marcia did not ask him anything about Buddy Pal. Then, with a kind of grim fatalism, she said, "I knew this all along, of course."

"Your heart told you," he said.

"Or some organ," she said. She turned and walked back to the bedroom, and a little later he arced his cigarette butt into the pool and followed.

"It was a wonderful wedding," I say.

I sit and smile in the sunlight, remembering. It was a lovely white chapel in Santa Monica; it had been used in the movies more than once to suggest firm, small-town American values. It had that traditional shape, the narrow front with the arched doors, the clapboard wall angling inward on both sides above the doors, then straightening again to reach upward, forming the steeple. In front of this setting, the gray cement walk came out straight and true from the front steps, flanked by gleaming green grass, mowed as tightly as a golf course. Two dozen clean and presentable well-wishers waited on this walk and this grass for Marcia and me to emerge from the chapel, hitched. On the fringes, a few reporters and photographers hovered, waiting to record the event.

I smile upon the dour interviewer; even upon him I smile. "I really believe," I tell him, "that first weddings are very important. They set the whole tone for your marriages to come. Buddy flew out from New York, of course,

60

to be best man, and Marcia's public-relations man set up the whole thing with a great deal of care and taste. The media were there, and the whole scene played just terrific."

I can still see it, in fact. Out of the chapel we came at the end of the ceremony, Jack Pine and Marcia "The First Mrs. Pine" Callahan. The gathered well-wishers crowded around us, wishing us well. Buddy came grinning out behind us, along with Marcia's PR man's secretary, the matron of honor. Rice was thrown. The driver got out of the white stretch limo waiting at the curb and opened the rear door. Photographers took pictures. We made our way, laughing and happy, through the laughing and happy throng. At the limo, Marcia turned and threw her bouquet. One of the female well-wishers caught it and squealed, and the other female well-wishers congratulated her with happy envy. Marcia and I waved and turned and entered the limo. It was swell!

I say to the interviewer, "We didn't know anybody on the Coast then, of course, so we hired a crowd from Central Casting, and those kids just did a super job. Later, some of them became personal friends."

The interviewer stares at me. "You mean, the whole scene was a fake?"

"Certainly not," I tell him. These little nobodies never understand a thing, you ever notice that? "The emotions expressed that day," I assure this little nobody, "were absolutely real. And if some real nice kids, swell young talents struggling to make it, could earn a dollar wishing us well as we launched ourselves onto the sea of matrimony, what's wrong with that? Good for their income, good for our image, good for the press, good for the people who read that kind of thing—well, *you* know that—good for everybody."

"I never looked at it like that," the interviewer confesses. But he still looks dubious.

"You have to see the big picture," I tell him gently, trying to be kind.

"I guess so," he says.

Well, how can you explain it? You had to be there. You had to look out the rear window of the limo the way I did as we drove away and see Buddy bring that big wad of bills out of his pocket, and see the happy expressions on all those swell young kids as they lined up on the church lawn to be paid. You don't think they were sincere?

"Anyway," I say, nodding, my mind brimful of fuzzy drink and fuzzy memories, "that was the best part of our marriage, the wedding. After that, it was pretty much all downhill, though I didn't know it at first."

"You didn't know you were having trouble in your own marriage?"

"Well," I say, brushing the back of one hand across my brow, feeling how the fuzzy drink presses against my skull, called to by your friend and mine, Big Sol, old Mister Sun, "well," I say, "I was pretty much concentrating on my career then. Or lack of career, I should say."

"Things didn't go well, at first, in Hollywood?"

"You could put it that way," I tell him, since he just did put it that way. "I had my New York reviews, my regional reviews, but no movie credits, and I just couldn't figure out what to do next, careerwise. Ever have one of those years where you just can't seem to get started?"

"No, sir," he says—of *course* he says!—and looks solemn and wimpish, gazing at me over his notebook (how *full* that notebook must be getting) as he says, "I don't believe I ever have had a year like that."

"Well, I have," I say, and nod, and decide it's better not to nod, and stop. "It's no fun, believe me," I say, and bring a shimmering hand up to my shimmering forehead.

"I'm sure it is," he agrees. Being polite, the little bastard.

"If I'd stayed in the theater," I say, and my hand waves in front of me in a negative way, outward, in a stop-frame sequence, the individual shots overlapping, the hand seeming to stay and to go, my life seeming to stay and to go, the career . . . "But," I say, and let it go at that.

Can't. The interviewer leans toward me, button eyes alight like a minor character in a minor sequel to *The*

Wizard of Oz. Tick-Tock and the Interviewer of Oz. I must perform.

"Oh, well," I say. "All right. I did some Shakespeare, regional things, some Molière, Mosca in a 'Volpone' in St. Louis they're *still* cackling over, but there's no coherence out there in the provinces, no career. You're not building anything; you aren't even making a living. Unemployment insurance—at a certain age, unemployment insurance can begin to seem like a sign of potential failure, you know what I mean?"

Is there a ghost of a smile hovering around my ghost of an interviewer's lips? Have I reached him on a human-to-human level yet again, man-to-man, soul-to-soul? Christ, what a thought. "Here's the thing of it," I say. "I had my reviews, I had my comparisons with Booth and Burton, but I wasn't *going* anywhere. Jack Schullmann was not a man to forgive and forget—well, few agents are—so every time my career seemed to come to life in some place like Minneapolis or Miami, he made sure to piss on it all over again back in New York. And theater *is* New York, it just is, no matter how much anybody else tries, anywhere at all. They build these theaters, flies that could fly a battleship, lightboards God would envy, and it doesn't matter. They could hire me and love me, weep when I wept, laugh when I laughed, die when I died, but it didn't matter, because the provinces never hear about *each other*, except through New York. And back in New York, there was Jack Schullmann, sitting on me, farting in my face."

"That's terrible," my interviewer says, whether at the fact or the image I do not know.

"I suppose I should have been able to outwait it," I say, "or walk away from it, but *how could I*? Acting was the only thing I had, the only thing that *used* me. I'd sell my soul to act," I say, and hear myself saying it, and laugh: "Well, I did, didn't I? But not to Jack Schullmann. He wasn't buying, not then."

"Does he still feel that way?" my interviewer asks,

"Uh-huh." The interviewer seems to think for a minute, brooding over his notebook like someone with something to hatch. Then he says, "So you came to Hollywood?"

I don't get it. Confused, I say, "Hollywood?" thinking of those miserable little houses on Woodrow Wilson Drive, with their miserable little swimming pools taking up the whole back yard. Why would anybody want to—?

Then I *do* get it. "Oh!" I say. "L*A*! Here, you mean. No, my college professor sent me to some fruit he knew in New York, an acting teacher. My folks said they'd give me a year, then I was on my own. That's the only time, really, for any length of time, the only time Buddy and I were ever separated."

"He didn't go to New York?"

"He went to the marines."

thereby disclosing not the depths of his research, but its shallowness. This guy doesn't know diddly about showbiz.

"Jack Schullmann died a few years ago," I say, smiling at the memory. "I sent a pizza to the funeral."

He stares at me. "You didn't."

"I did. SO LONG, PAL, was spelled out on it, in provolone. By then, of course, we loved each other; I was too big for him to hate. He had to love me for the sake of clients I might want to work with. But back in the early days, it was a different story. And it wasn't just Jack, either. It was his friends, too, and Miriam's old friends—*thee-ah-tah* friends, you know. They wouldn't walk down the *block* past a theater I was working in. So it was LA or nothing."

"The usual story about fine actors, the way I've always heard it," my interviewer says, rather disconcertingly suggesting that his boringly round little head might contain ideas of its own after all, "is that the movies seduce them away from what might have been great stage careers."

"There *are* no great stage careers, not anymore," I tell him. "And nobody seduced me into the movies. In fact, at first, nobody *wanted* me in the movies. It wasn't a blacklist out here, it was just indifference. My own, too. I was worn out, I was losing faith in my talent, I didn't know what to do or how to start all over." I smile reminiscently. "I owe my stardom to Marcia, really," I say, demonstrating my world-renowned generosity. "She encouraged me in those darkest hours."

FLASHBACK 9A

On her way home from the studio, Marcia picked up her and Jack's dry cleaning, then continued on up and over Beverly Glen Boulevard out of the Valley and into Westwood to the furnished rental she now shared with her husband. She thumbed the garage-opener button as she made the turn into her driveway, and the broad blank door folded up and back, accepting its daily diet of Porsche.

Marcia collected the plastic dry-cleaner bag, which had been draped over the back of the passenger seat, then climbed from the car, and went through the connecting door and through the kitchen and the corner of the living room and down the hall, the dry-cleaner bag held over her shoulder like Frank Sinatra's jacket. Walking down the hall, Marcia glanced leftward and saw, in profile, Jack.

Still there. In the same old cowboy hat and fringed jacket and high decorated boots, he sat in his favorite canvas chair at the deep end of the pool, seated well down and back so his head and knees were at the same height, cowboy hat pulled low over his eyes to shade them from the afternoon sun, booted legs stretched far out in front of him over the redwood deck with ankles crossed, hands folded casually in lap. From a cigarette in the corner of his mouth, a slender pale tendril of smoke wavered upward past his ear and the brim of his hat.

Marcia did not break stride. Her eyes narrowed slightly, she gazed steadily at that self-absorbed profile out there, and she kept walking, on down to the end of the hall, where she faced front again at last, moving through the doorway into the master bedroom.

Clean laundry stood in neat folded piles on the bed. Nodding as though to say her expectations had been fulfilled, she walked around the bed to the wall of closets and hung the dry-cleaning bag on the rod. Then she turned, looked again at the laundry on the bed, took a long, slow breath, and glanced across the room at her reflection in the dresser mirror there. No expression showed in the face looking back at her.

Marcia stepped through the sliding glass door to the outside, slid it shut behind her, and stood at the shallow end of the pool, looking down across the water at Jack, who hadn't moved. An almost inaudible sigh parted her lips, which then pressed shut again. Deliberately she strode around the pool; he finally—as she was halfway to him—lifted his head and lifted his hand to lift his cowboy hat away from his eyes to watch her. Nothing else on him moved.

Marcia stopped in front of him. They looked at each other for a long silent moment, and then, with a kind of grim fatalism, she said, "Get off your dead ass."

"Hi, honey," he said mildly, a happy smile playing at the corners of his lips. "How'd things go today at the studio?"

She shook her head, pushing that aside, saying, "What did *you* do today?"

He considered. "Well," he said, "the laundry."

"Jack," she said, "you've got to get *out* of this house, you've got to get *moving*, you've got to get your life *going* again. Do you want to spend the rest of your life as a kept man?"

He considered that question, giving it careful thought, and then a sunny smile glowed all over his face and he looked up at her and said, "Yes!"

"No!" she told him, and pointed a rigid finger at his nose. "You," she said, "are going to get a job."

Mildly, the smile still faintly lighting his features, he gazed up at her, blinking.

So Marcia got me an appointment with her agent, Irwin Sandstone, a man who had guided lots of fellas just like me to movie stardom.

FLASHBACK 10

The views were magnificent, or would have been, if Los Angeles had anything magnificent to look at. From this corner office high in one of the silvery godless megaliths of Century City, one view was northward across the smog and over the boxy little houses in peach and coral toward the low but steep hills serving as the only redan against the proles of the Valley, while the other view was westward over flatter and peachier but less smoggy Santa Monica toward the eternal Pacific. Just down that way to the left lurked Venice, waiting for a far-sighted developer.

The office had been decorated with an eye to the exudation of casual power: relaxed, but potent, the spider's parlor as a philosophical statement through the art of interior design. In this light, well-cleaned space, Jack Pine sat transfixed on a beautiful but uncomfortable chair in the middle of the room while Irwin Sandstone paced slowly around him. Irwin Sandstone, a pear-shaped man with a bald-headed toad's face and a scalloped wrinkling of the ears, held a small slender bronze art deco figure of a naked, nubile girl in the short, stuffed fingers of his hands. As he walked, and as he talked, he fondled this statue, the light gleaming from his rings and from the clear nail polish his manicurist had assured him no one would notice. He said:

"Your career is important to me, Jack. And the reason your career is important to me is because it's unique. If I wanted to be in the shoe business, eight million shoes all the same, I'd be in the shoe business. The business I'm in, this crazy mad business of show business, not shoe business, in which I thank God I've had a certain modicum of success, in this business, every new face, every new body, every new voice, every new talent that comes through that door is a separate and unique challenge, another opportunity for me to prove myself. Do you know what I mean, Jack?"

"I think so, sir," Jack said. Today he wore brown loafers and tan chinos and a polo shirt with an alligator on it and an open, welcoming, guileless expression.

Irwin Sandstone's blunt thumb caressed the statue's budding breasts. "I am a mere servant of the creative impulse, Jack," he said, circling and circling. "It's *your* unique gift we're concerned with here, not the life or goals or dreams of Irwin Sandstone."

"Yes, sir," said Jack.

Irwin's fingers oiled and warmed the bronze. "How to mold, how to shape, how to bring out to the acclaim of the multitudes that unique talent deep within you, *that* is my humble duty, that is my mantra, to serve great talents, to be the willing stepping stone on which they rise, to do whatever is within my small powers"—with a wave at the power-reeking office—"to bring each wonderful unique private talent to its greatest glory. That is what I wish to do with *you*, Jack. *If* you agree. Will you give me that task, Jack? Will you order me to make you great?"

Accommodating, Jack said, "Sure."

Suddenly more businesslike, clutching the statue's legs, Irwin nodded. "Okay," he said, and stood still, to Jack's left, appraising him, nodding slowly to himself, while Jack struggled to decide whether he was supposed to meet Irwin Sandstone's gaze frankly or face forward to be studied. Compromising, he faced more or less forward, and flicked constant glances toward the man hefting him in his mind.

"Okay," Irwin Sandstone said again, the statue forgotten, its head in his fist. "For your type," he said, "we start with the biker picture, then your pathologic killer, then your patient picture. By then you're established, you can do whatever you want."

Jack, manfully smiling, said, "Patient picture?"

Irwin Sandstone negligently waved the hand with the statue in it. "Nut house or hospital," he explained. "You're a person with an affliction, see? Gives you that human dimension, rounds you off after the psycho."

"Oh, yeah," Jack said. "I see what you mean."

Irwin Sandstone brought his hands together. They found the statue again, apparently on their own, and the fat fingers stroked and fumbled as their owner gazed appealingly at Jack to say, "Is that what you want, Jack? Stardom? Fruition? Will you put yourself in my hands?"

Jack watched those hands fondle the thin bronze girl. He shrugged. "What have I got to lose?" he said.

LUDE

O'Connor watches the movie star seated on his gray slate patio in his pale blue terry-cloth robe, vaguely smiling, ignoring the sounds from the swimming pool right nearby. He's good at ignoring things, O'Connor thinks.

The reminiscence of the introduction to Irwin Sandstone floats in the lambent air, dissipates like opium smoke in the sun. After a little silence, the famous Jack Pine sleepily says, "Irwin was the genius, not me, and we both knew it." Slowly he is arching backward, body collapsing gradually onto the slates. Lying there, blind-looking eyes gazing skyward, voice fading more and more, "But Irwin came thruuuuuuuuuu," Pine murmurs. "Ahh-hhhhh, I'll give himmmmmm . . ."

The eyes close. He has drifted off, his breathing deep and even. O'Connor waits a moment, memo pad in left hand, pencil in right, but the actor doesn't alter in any way. At last, O'Connor leans forward from his chair, extends his right arm forward, taps the sleeping star on the knee with the eraser end of his pencil. "Mister Pine?" he says. "Sir?"

No response.

Abruptly, the stone-faced butler, Hoskins, appears with a silver tray bearing a glass full of oily black muck. "Allow me to help, sir," he says.

"He's all yours," O'Connor says, and leans back in his canvas chair again to watch.

Hoskins goes to one knee, places the silver tray on the slate beside himself, props the actor up against his raised knee with practiced ease, pinches the actor's nose between thumb and forefinger of left hand, and with the right hand pours the glassful of oily black muck down Jack Pine's throat.

O'Connor winces, empathizing despite himself. He says, "Does this happen a lot, Hoskins?"

Still pouring, the viscous fluid slowly oozing from the glass into the unconscious man's mouth, Hoskins says, "We have an amazing amount and variety of chemicals in our body, sir. Maintaining the balance is not at all easy."

"I can see that," O'Connor says.

The glass is now mostly empty, only an oily metallic coating still staining its sides. Hoskins puts the glass back on the tray, and lowers the body to the slate. Then he picks up the tray, stands, and says, "We should be coming around any instant, sir."

With which, the actor *pops* upright, sitting at attention, legs straight out in front, arms stretched out and back behind him like flying buttresses. His eyes are wide open. "Hoskins!" he cries.

Hoskins bows a deferential head in his direction. "Sir?"

Speaking at incredible speed, Pine says, "I've got it! We'll put white pillars every seven feet all around the side, and put the lawn on *top*, and then we can go underneath when it's too sunny!"

"Interesting, sir," Hoskins says. As Pine's head twitches back and forth, his wide eyes staring here and there like a demented bird, Hoskins stoops, picks up the empty glass that once contained the fuzzy drink, puts it beside the black muck glass on the tray, nods at O'Connor, and departs, walking ramrod-stiff toward the house.

Pine's darting head and staring eyes find O'Connor, gawk at him. Pine giggles. He points at O'Connor, teetering on only one buttress, giggling with accomplishment, with his own discovery. *"People!"* he cries.

O'Connor, bewildered, looks around and then points the pencil at himself, saying, "No, sir, it's just me. Like before."

"People magazine," Jack Pine says, nodding, smiling, cackling. "The cover *again!"*

How much longer can the actor possibly believe this is a press interview? O'Connor sighs, and waits.

Hello, hello, here I am again, just fine, doing just fine, everything's just—

Hello, here I am again. I'm back with it now, it's back with me now, my with now is it—

Hello. There's something terribly wrong here, call a priest. No, wait. Maybe better not.

Hello?

Here I am. Lost myself for a while, fell down some rabbit hole—"I'm late, I'm late," as my girlfriends used to say— fell down some black nasty . . . Dead? *Who's* dead?

Hello?

I gaze about me, and the interviewer sits patiently, sits watching me, sits patiently watching me. "Hello," I say.

"Hello," he says. "Are you all right?"

"Jes fine," I say.

"And you remember—"

"The story of my life," I tell him, "in its endlessly unreeling permutations. I remember now. Where exactly were we in the sequence of events?"

"Your new agent," he says, reading from his notes, "had told you to start with a biker picture."

"Precisely so!" I say, delighted to be on track again. *So* inconvenient to fade in and out like that, I really must talk to my doctors about it, find some different formulation— No; they'll all just use those dread words:

Cut.

Down.

And the hell you say, doc. I didn't come this far to *cut down*. Not me. "Shit!" I cry, staring at the interviewer, who looks more and more like a fish in a sports jacket. "I've lost it again," I confess.

"Biker picture," he says.

"That's it! Okay! All right, the biker was shot in the studio, came out exactly the way we wanted. I mean *exactly* the way we wanted: a crowd churner but a stomach pleaser as well, good gross, good reviews, good first step."

"Sounds good," the interviewer says.

Is he trying to be *funny*? I peer sharply at him, but he's as deadpan as ever, dead fish in a pan. "Right," I say. "Anyway, next was the pathologic killer, and that involved six weeks' location in Mexico. My first time out of the country. Marcia had another picture then, up here, so down there I went, all on my own. Money in my pocket. Fame starting. Travel in foreign lands. Starring in a movie! I told Buddy, up here, before I got on the plane, I said, 'My dreams are coming true before I dream them.'"

The interviewer actually brightens up; he looks actually pleased for me. "That must be terrific," he says.

"That's just what it is. That's just what it is. But then, what happened next . . ."

    *
    *
    *
    *
    *
    *
    *
    *
    *

*

*

"Mr. Pine?"

*

*

*

"Mr. Pine?"

"Nuhh?

"You were in Mexico. What happened next, you said."

"Oh, what happened next. Yeah." I make a smile. "Midway through, down there, my leading lady got laryngitis, couldn't scream at all for five days. I took the opportunity to rush home and see my darling Marcia."

FLASHBACK 11

Having two salaries now, blessed with growing reputations, Mr. and Mrs. Jack Pine could afford, in fact needed, a larger house, a more prestigious location, better suited to greeting friends and the press. This house, until recently owned by a television star named Holt who'd committed suicide when his series was canceled, sprawled on three levels, a white blob cunningly worked into a fold of canyon up near Mulholland Drive. Though the view was of the Valley, the approach was from the Los Angeles side, and the area code was 213, not (gulp) 818.

The box hooked to the visor of Jack's rented BMW operated the gate at the end of the cul-de-sac off Mulholland, where their driveway began. He drove in, the gate swinging sidearm shut behind him, and steered around the carefully jungly plantings to the sudden blacktop puddle where the house began; three-car attached garage on the right, entrance and main living room straight ahead.

Gathering up his same old two pieces of luggage—the

battered round, soft traveling bag and the well-worn soft suit-carrier—Jack unlocked his way into the house. He crossed the large formal living room with its large formal view of the Valley nestling its large blanket of dirty gray haze, and went down the stairs to level two, with its more informal family room and bedrooms all opening onto the large free-form pool, which sparkled and gleamed below the sightline of the formal view above. Coming into the large comfortable family room with its conversation pit and its walls graced with rented original oil paintings, Jack looked around with pride of ownership and the happiness of contentment. This was his; his and Marcia's.

The television set was on, showing *Bringing Up Baby*. A large book of the paintings of Hopper lay on the broad glass coffee table, open to "Nighthawks." Beside the book were a half-full coffee cup and a half-eaten sandwich. Jack looked at all these things, his smile quizzical, then dropped his luggage and crossed the room to feel the coffee cup. It was warm.

His smile broadening, Jack tiptoed across the room and opened the hall door. Tiptoeing past the rented framed etchings, he couldn't help a conspiratorial chuckle.

The master bedroom door was at the end, on the right. It was closed. Jack reached it, closed his hand around the doorknob, hesitated once more, grinning, and then leaped through the doorway, yelling, "Surprise!"

Buddy reared up in the bed, looking over his shoulder in amazement and shock. Beneath him, Marcia writhed. "Not *noowww!*" she wailed. "I'm coming!"

Jack stood in the bedroom where his momentum had left him. Turned to stone, he stared into Buddy's eyes. He could neither speak nor move.

Buddy was horribly embarrassed, achingly aware of the social awkwardness of the situation in which they all found themselves. But he was quite obviously also aware of the woman still desperately thrashing away beneath him. He offered Jack a ghastly smile, saying, "Give us a minute, will you, Dad, uh, just a minute, we'll . . ."

An electric jolt shot through Jack's body, slamming him

back into life. Spinning about, he flung himself from the room, the door banging behind him with a sound like a shot. "Nice to see you, Dad, uh . . ." Buddy called after him, in despairing camaraderie.

"Oh, *there* it is," Marcia gasped, her hands clutching his shoulder blades. "Oh, there it is, oh, there it is, oh, there it is."

"There it is, all right," Buddy muttered, broody.

Marcia's breathing slowed, her arms relaxed, she raised her head beside Buddy's and looked toward the door. Lank hair plastered to her skin framed her face. Still panting a bit, beginning to look worried, she said, "Was that Jack?"

"Mmmmmm," Buddy said, meaning *yes*.

From far away came the sound of a car engine roaring, the accelerator pressed ridiculously to the floor. Then there was the grinding sound of some sort of crash, a tiny pause, and once again that roaring sound, this time receding to silence.

"What was that?" said Marcia.

"Jack's going," Buddy said.

The interviewer glares at me in prissy disapproval. "There you go again," he says. "You didn't *see* that part. You were driving away."

"With a broken heart," I say. "Plus two broken headlights and a cracked radiator. But one senses the truth of such scenes, doesn't one? One doesn't have to be *present* at every fucking instance of an emotional scene to sense the reality when one fucking well hears it, *does* one?"

"Okay, okay," he says, patting the air at me. "Take it easy, Mr. Pine. It's your story."

"My wife and my best friend," I say, with my best brokenhearted chuckle. "The oldest story in the world, am I right?"

"Second oldest, I think," he says, nit-picking again.

"Old, though," I say, too weary to fight. "Very old. Buddy came to see me in Mexico."

FLASHBACK 12

The hot Mexican sun beat down on an old Mexican village: adobe walls, brown earth street, flat bleaching light. Jack, dressed in dirty black pants, black leather jacket, and white shirt buttoned to the collar, stalked cautiously along next to the wall, a six-inch bowie knife held at the ready in his hand, out in front of him, swaying like a snake to left and right. All at once a small Mexican boy, barefoot, in ragged shirt and pants, came whistling around the corner into Jack's path, paying attention to nothing. Seeing the knife, seeing Jack, he let out a bloodcurdling shriek and, as Jack lunged uselessly at him with the knife, the boy scrambled back around the corner and out of sight. Jack straightened, lowering the knife, and leaned his free hand wearily against the wall.

"Okay, Jack," came the amplified voice of the director. "Very nice. But the kid came in a little late."

The kid came back around the corner of the false wall in this false mockup of a corner of a Mexican town out of *Juarez*, and frowned irritably in the direction of the director and all the technicians and the black hulks of the machines, haloed by the powerful lights assisting the sun. Out of character, it could be seen that the kid was a kid, but not a Mexican. With the impatience of the professional surrounded by amateurs, he said, "Who the heck's supposed to cue me around here? I finally went when I saw the guy's shadow."

The guy—that is, Jack—took no part in the ensuing discussion. He seemed muted, deadened. After a minute, when not given any further directions, he simply turned away on his own, knife hand dangling at his side, and plodded back to his starting position. As he did so, he glanced without interest toward the crew and equipment and stopped dead.

Buddy. In among it all, the camera, boom, sound equipment, lighting, grips, technicians, makeup man, script girl, stills photographer, visitors to the set, the whole shifting population of the village that lives just behind the camera, down there in the midst of them all stood Buddy. Jack's vision contracted; it was as though his sight had irised into a tight circle surrounded by black the way they used to point at information in silent movies. There was Buddy, in the circle of the iris, and all the rest of the world was black.

A tiny, tentative, sheepish, hesitant smile touched Buddy's lips. A tiny, tentative, sheepish little wave of his hand barely reached as high as his waist.

Jack gazed across the dusty tan intervening space. People in the other world were talking, moving around, living their lives; he was aware of none of it. He saw only Buddy. The left side of his upper lip lifted, curling back, showing a moist glint of tooth. Slowly, deep in his throat, a snarl began. It flowed from his mouth, growing, louder. All at once, Jack raised the bowie knife above his head, *bellowed* like an enraged bull, and leaped across that intervening space directly at his oldest friend in all the world.

People in that other world screamed and fled. Buddy, in this world, stared in horror at that knife but stayed rooted to the spot. Jack launched himself at Buddy like a tiger, the knife flashing in the sun, slashing down across Buddy's chest.

Buddy screamed. He recoiled, falling back a step, putting up his hands in a vain attempt to defend himself. Jack slashed with the knife, his arm raising and lowering, again and again, the blade gleaming and gleaming, until finally Buddy managed to push him away and back out of range, staggering, shocked, outraged. "Ow!" Buddy cried. "That hurts!"

Jack, out of breath, stood spraddle-legged in the dust where Buddy had pushed him, the knife hanging from his hand at his side. Face dulled again, he gazed bleakly at Buddy and panted like a dog on a summer day.

Meanwhile, Buddy was realizing he hadn't been cut. Looking down at himself, seeing no blood, seeing his clothes intact and not cut to ribbons, he stared in wonder and then pointed at the knife, saying, "What *is* that?"

A number of crew members, finally getting over their first shock, had now run forward to grasp the unresisting Jack by the arms and shoulders and waist. One of these men unbent Jack's unprotesting fingers and removed the knife from his grip. Holding it up, showing it to Buddy, he bent the blade back and forth, showing its resilience. "Rubber," he said.

"Well, it *hurts*," Buddy said, no longer frightened, beginning to be both embarrassed and aggrieved. Rubbing his arms and chest, he said, "I'm gonna be all over bruises."

The crew members turned the now-catatonic Jack and began to lead him away toward his dressing trailer. Buddy looked up, saw Jack leaving, and put out his hand, calling, "Stop! Wait! Let him go."

The group of men holding Jack stopped and turned around so Jack was facing Buddy again, but they didn't let him go. Stepping forward, speaking loudly enough for everyone present to hear him, Buddy said, "It's all right, it really is. I deserved that. I won't tell you what I did to this fine man, but I deserved even *more* than a rubber knife. I destroyed the finest friendship a man ever had."

Slowly Jack lifted his head. Slowly his eyes focused on Buddy, seeing him through a haze of despair. Slowly Buddy's words made their way into his brain.

Buddy stepped forward, closer to his old friend. The group holding Jack released him and faded away. Speaking more softly, Buddy said, "Nobody's ever had a finer friend than I had in Jack Pine."

Buddy's eyes locked on Jack's. Jack's eyes locked on Buddy's. Buddy said, with simple intensity, "I would have laid down my life for you, Dad, and I know you would have done the same for me."

Over behind the sound equipment, a fella with a guitar began softly to play a lonesome tune. With unembellished frankness, Buddy said, "We go back a long ways together, Jack Pine, a long ways. To the very beginning."

Jack raised his head, sunlight refracting from the despair in his eyes. Speaking from a throat as dry and dusty as the ground they stood on, he said, "That doesn't matter anymore, Buddy. Nothing matters anymore, not what anybody knows, not what anybody did. None of it matters, Buddy."

"You're right, Jack Pine," Buddy said. "In one careless, thoughtless moment of selfishness, I threw it all away. I didn't deserve your friendship, Jack Pine. I never did."

His passion spent, wanting nothing but to be alone in his trailer with his personal silence and darkness, Jack shook his head and made a vague gesture and said, "Oh, sure you did, Buddy. You deserved my friendship, sure you did. Lots of times."

"Never, Jack Pine," Buddy said. "Never."

Jack Pine was an actor. How could he help but get caught up in the mood of the scene? How could he help but begin to *feel* the emotion of the scene? How could he help but say, "You know what I owe you, Buddy Pal. *You* know, more than anyone else. I owe you my life, Buddy Pal. I owe you everything I have. You saved me back there when . . ."

screams, screaming, engine roars, flashing lights in red and white reflecting from the bumper chrome, slicking on the

85

heaving trunk of the car, madness, danger, movement, peril,
speed . . .

"Nnn-*ahhh*-ah!"

"Jack Pine!"

"Buddy Pal! Buddy Pal!" Back from terror, Jack stared
in dread at his oldest friend. "You *know*, Buddy Pal!" he
cried. "I owe you *everything*. Do you know what I mean?"

"But not *that*, Jack," Buddy insisted, shaking his head.
"Not to take *that* from you, Jack Pine. What I did in your
bed was unforgivable, I know it was. I know you can never
forgive me, and I know I don't deserve to be forgiven."

"But I *do* forgive you, Buddy," Jack said, raising hands
that trembled.

"You can't, Jack, you *can't*."

"I can, Buddy," Jack said, a crazed and holy smile
forming on his lips. "I can, and I do, and I will, and you
can't stop me. I forgive you!"

"Jack! Jack!"

"I forgive you, Buddy Pal! I forgive you!"

"Oh, Jack! Jack!"

Jack pulled Buddy into his arms. Tightly they embraced, eyes squeezed shut, faces buried in each other's
shoulders. A collective sigh rose from the semicircle of
assembled spectators. Strong men were seen to wipe away
a tear. Women were seen thoughtfully to lick a lip. The
guitar music flowed its mournful message. Then the applause started, slight at first, but growing, mingling with
the guitar.

Jack and Buddy reared back so they could see each
other, but still held tightly to each other's arms. Both men
were crying for happiness. The applause continued, and
beneath it Buddy said, his voice throbbing with sincerity,
"But the most important person to forgive, Jack Pine, is
your little Marcia."

Weeping, tears and makeup commingling on his face,
Jack shook his head. "Buddy, Buddy," he said, "you don't
know what you're asking."

"She needs you, Jack Pine," Buddy told him. "Your little
Marcia needs you."

"Oh, no, she doesn't," Jack said, his voice hardening.

"Oh, yes, she does," Buddy said. "She's going to have your baby."

I wipe away a tear. Then I taste it. It tastes like the sea. I think I like the sea better than I like swimming pools. I think I don't like swimming pools the way I used to. I smile sadly—I feel myself doing it, smiling sadly—I smile sadly at the interviewer and I say, "That was the last time Buddy and I ever fought about anything."

He seems surprised. As though challenging me, he says, "The last time?"

But it's the truth, the simple truth. All truth is simple. "The last time," I say.

"And Marcia Callahan was pregnant with your first child at that time?"

Less simple. "The blood test was inconclusive," I say. "But when Buddy brought me the news, what could I do? I went back to the nasty bitch. And you know the first thing I said to her?"

"What was that?"

FLASHBACK 13

The shades were drawn against the California sun. In the rose-colored light in the same bedroom in which Jack found that awful scene, Jack and Marcia lay in bed, half-covered by wrinkled sheets, both warm, perspiring, Marcia in a glow of reconciliation, Jack puffing on a cigarette as he lay half-propped against the soft headboard, Marcia's head against his shoulder. He turned her face toward his, and she gazed up at him with melting eyes. His free hand smoothed her hair as he looked deep into those eyes. Gently, he said, "He better look a lot like me."

"And did he?"

I shrug; a dangerous gesture. Perhaps a simple and dignified nod in future. But now I shrugged, and recovered, and I say, "She was a girl. Took after her mother, in fact, in more ways than one."

"Let's see," the interviewer says, annoyingly tapping his pencil against his notebook as he gazes out over my head and over the swimming pool behind me and into the middle distance. "That would be your daughter Rosalia, wouldn't it?"

"That's right." I grin the grin I used when I played Satan that time. "I named her after a lady in Mexico that helped me during the movie down there."

The interviewer nods and reels in his glance to look again at me, saying, "How old would she be now?"

"Well, she *would* be about thirty-five," I say, "but the fact is she's nineteen. Last I heard, she's living in Colombia with some big dope dealer down there." I feel a crooked and half-proud grin coming to my lips. I say, "Smart for a kid of mine, huh? Cuts out the middleman."

"You and Marcia Callahan had three children together, didn't you?"

This time I remember not to shrug. I perform a simple and dignified nod. I say, "She had three kids while we were married. I suppose I had something to do with it. But the marriage, you know, never really did survive that first big shock."

"Even after Buddy Pal came to Mexico to try to make things up with you?"

"Didn't matter," I say. "It's a funny thing, but I really *did* forgive Buddy. We got to be best friends again just as though nothing had ever happened. But I never in my heart forgave Marcia. I guess in *her* heart she must have known that. She was never stupid, the bitch."

"And all," the interviewer says, "because of one simple mistake."

"Well, at least one. But also, there was our careers. The movie of *Tupelo* didn't do business, and you know what that means out here. They blame everybody but the producer, and Marcia got her share of the debit. After that, her career just sort of stuttered along for a while, so-so roles in nothing pictures, no build-up, just the gradual realization on everybody's part that the industry could get along just as well without her."

"Tough on her, I guess."

"You bet. Particularly because, for me, it went just the other way. I hit with the biker, consolidated with the pathological killer, and got my first Oscar nomination with the patient picture."

"*Slip of the Knife*," the interviewer says, nodding yet again at the brilliance of his own research.

"Yeah, that's right. That's the picture where I first really got it together, my own talent and the technology of film. Where the camera and I blended into one creature, one omnivorous animal that could eat *anything* and not die. *Slip of the Knife*; that's when I hit my stride, got a bridle and bit on my powers, *became* the superstar. After *Slip of the Knife*, I was one of those very few stars that could do anything at all and the people still come, they pay the money, they sit down, they watch. I could read the phone book and they'd come. I could read the *Valley* phone book and they'd come."

"I guess that's true," he says, thoughtfully, as though it hadn't occurred to him before why *he* should be interviewing *me*.

"It is," I assure him. I stretch my arms and legs, bend from the waist. My entire skeleton aches. What have I been doing with this body, this instrument of my talent? Fucking it over, man.

And worse. I suspect, I suspect worse.

No no no, there are things I must not know.

Do not look toward the swimming pool.

Patiently my interviewer sits, awaiting the dropping of further pearls from these lips, and so I oblige him. "After *Slip of the Knife*," I tell him, "just like Irwin said, I could do anything I wanted, the industry was mine. I had to hire a girl just to read the scripts they sent me. As for Marcia, well, around town, more and more she was getting to be known as Mrs. Jack Pine, with fewer and fewer parts coming her way. She couldn't stand that. So, one day, when Rosalia was four and Indira was two and Little Buddy was five months . . ."

FLASHBACK 14

This living room, large and airy, expensively and artfully furnished in shades of gray and blond and white, with *owned* original oil paintings on the walls, was up in the hills of Beverly Hills. The view out the large but well-curtained windows was of green hillsides tastefully decorated with mansions. Jack, in cashmere pullover and flannel slacks, barefoot, strolled up and down the thick pile shag rug, studying a movie script, silently mouthing his lines. In his other hand was a bottle of Tuborg beer from which he occasionally sipped.

Marcia entered from deeper in the house, wearing a well-tailored gray suit and a small hat with a veil. She looked elegant and handsome, but older. She was pulling on suede gloves. She stood a moment watching Jack, but he remained absorbed in his script, pacing back and forth, lips moving, expressions flowing and changing on his face.

At last Marcia moved over directly in his path and watched without expression as he paced away from her, swiveled, and came pacing back. Even then he might have simply angled around her if she hadn't, in a low and cold and emotionless voice, said "Jack?"

He stopped in front of her. He looked up inquiringly from his script. Marcia reared back and gave him an open-handed walloping roundhouse gloved right across the face. The script went flying. The Tuborg bottle went flying. Jack himself went flying, backward and over the nearest low white suede sofa.

Marcia waited, adjusting her right glove, face still expressionless, until Jack righted himself on the floor over there and his bewildered face appeared above the sofa back. Then she nodded. "Good-bye," she said.

Open-mouthed, Jack watched her stride across the living room and out the front door. His slack jaw, the left side of it reddening, rested on the cool suede of the sofa back.

I lean forward. Elbow resting on my interviewer's gray-clad, bony, silently protesting knee, I reminiscently rub my jaw, where the ghost of Marcia's departing hand still shimmers and burns. With two fingers and thumb, I check the working of my jaw hinge. All aches are psychosomatic, aren't they?

I can tell my interviewer is feeling sympathetic at this moment because, though his face remains frozen in that blank look of reception, he is not pushing my elbow off his person. He is restraining his prissiness. Even to the extent of letting sympathy seep into his voice as he says, "She left you just like that, huh? No warning, no discussion, just up and walked out, just like that."

"Just like that," I agree. "She took the kids. Boy, the books *they'll* write some day."

"And they're all still in their teens."

"The Sargasso Sea of the teens," I say. "In their teens. The penal colony of the teens. I remember my tee— No, I don't! Memory begone!"

"There's something back there, isn't there?" my interviewer asks me. "Something that explains everything that followed. That's what it's all about, isn't it?"

This knee is too bony, too gray-clad, too prissy. I withdraw my friendly elbow, I turn away—*not* toward the pool!—I turn back, I find my place on the teleprompter of my eyelids, I say, "Marcia."

"Yes?"

"She left."

"Yes."

"I gave her the house, three pints of blood, and Ventnor Avenue, and after that Buddy and I moved into a place out on the beach."

"Buddy again? Just the two of you?"

"Heck, no," I say, smiling at the memory. Well, the beginning of the memory, anyway. "I got to fulfill an old dream. I brought my mom and dad out to live with me."

FLASHBACK 15

The bedroom was small and square, with off-white walls and blond wood floor and very prominent electric outlets, prominent because the room was not yet furnished. The only objects in it were two white wooden kitchen chairs without arms, facing each other. On one stood a portable TV set, its black wire reaching back to a cable outlet low on the wall. To one side, plate-glass doors showed a broad gray wood deck in blinding sunlight, with the broad gray Pacific heaving like chicken soup beyond.

The room's interior door—flush, painted white—opened and Jack entered, smiling, sweating, awkward, trying to please, ushering in his mom and dad. Mom was short and buxom, round-faced, jolly; she wore an old print dress and a gray cardigan. Her hands were full of snapshots. Dad, short and skinny and dry, wore white shirt and black pants and shoes, all too big for him. His face had a collapsed look around the mouth.

"And this is *your* room!" Jack exclaimed, pumping up his enthusiasm, giving one of the very few poor performances of his acting career. Gesturing madly at the bare walls, the white chairs, the ocean outside, he said, "Furniture's going to be delivered by noon! All brand new!"

Mom had been waiting impatiently for Jack to shut up or at least pause for a breath. When he finally did so, she shuffled toward him, holding up snapshots, saying, "Here's cousin Rosie with the twins. And here's the twins with Blair's dog. And this is the Flynns' new car."

"TV," Dad said.

As Jack smiled and nodded and stared glaze-eyed at Mom's photographs, Buddy entered, smiling, hands clasped in front of him, nodding like the co-host he was, and Dad crossed the room to switch on the television set and seat himself expectantly on the edge of the other chair.

"Great reception here, Dad," Jack told him.

The picture blossomed on the screen. Dad leaned forward to start switching channels.

Mom held up more snapshots. "Here's the laurel tree out behind Margaret's house. Look how it's grown! Can you see, Jack?"

Jack tore his eyes away from the back of Dad's head. As Dad went on switching among the channels, Jack looked at the picture of the laurel tree out behind Margaret's house. "Yeah, gosh," he said. "Sure has grown."

"You look, too, Buddy," Mom said.

"Okay, Mom Pine." Buddy obediently leaned forward, gazing with pleased interest at the picture of the laurel tree out behind Margaret's house.

Dad, his voice testy, his manner testy, even his shoulder blades testy, said, "Where's the sports?"

Grinning spastically, like a lion tamer who's just heard a low growl from behind him, Jack said, "There might not be any sports right now, Dad."

Dad stopped switching channels, sat back with an air of triumph, and pointed at the set. "Wrong again, Sonny. Tennis."

"That's nice," Jack said.

"There, now," Mom said, "just leave your father to his sports. We'll all go sit on the sofa and look at pictures."

"Okay, Mom Pine," Buddy said.

Jack flashed a dozen smiles toward his father's impervious profile. "See you later, Dad."

Dad ignored him. Mom hustled the two younger men out of the room and firmly shut the door. Sunshine bleached the world beyond the glass doors. Dad watched tennis.

Sunshine bleaches the world. I sit beneath it, the white light making haloes and auras and ghosts and spirits in my vision. "I introduced Mom and Dad to all my industry friends," I tell my interviewer, "and they fit right in."

FLASHBACK 15A

The concept of the living room in the Malibu house was casual living with plenty of room to entertain friends. In an open central fireplace built on a platform of white brick, a cozy fire crackled. Comfortable furniture of canvas and wood, easily maintained and quite weatherproof, stood back out of the way so that the forty people at the party could flow around the fireplace and in and out of the broad doorways leading to the sunstruck deck. A good third of the partygoers wore famous names and famous faces, and most of the rest were their associates: wives, agents, boyfriends, attorneys. Uniformed staff passed discreetly through the crowd with canapés and drinks.

To one side of it all stood Jack, viewing the scene with sweaty pride. He watched his mom, in the same print dress and gray cardigan as before, move around the room, buttonholing people, clutching their elbows, showing them photograph after photograph, her victims all being distracted but polite. He watched his dad, in a far corner, seated with his back to the crowd, watching "Bowling for

Dollars" on a large, elaborate console TV. He watched Buddy perched on the back of a sofa, drink in hand, easy and aggressive smile on face, chatting up a pretty girl in a summer dress.

Dad leaned forward and unceremoniously shoved at the hip of a male partygoer who had drifted backward partway between Dad and the TV set. The partygoer looked around in surprise, saw what he'd done, apologized, and moved away.

Mom, her hands full of snapshots, pursued a distinguished older gentleman—the only man there in a suit—out onto the deck under the sun.

Buddy rose from the sofa, took the pretty girl by the elbow, and walked her over to Dad and the TV set. "Dad Pine," he said, "I'd like you to meet—"

With a warning cough, not really a groan or a snarl, Dad said, "Bud-dy."

"Dad Pine," Buddy said easily, unintimidated, "that's the commercial. Come on, I want you to meet a very nice girl. Annie, this is Jack's father."

"Hi," said the pretty girl to the back of Dad's head.

Dad swiveled around, still irritable, and looked past Buddy at the pretty girl. He reacted with surprise, and then with pleasure, and popped to his feet. Smiling at the pretty girl, he reached into his shirt pocket and brought out a full set of false teeth. Still smiling at the pretty girl, he inserted these teeth into his mouth, wiped his right hand on his pants to dry it somewhat, and extended it toward her, now flashing a smile full of gleaming teeth. "Nice to know you," he said.

Glazed, the pretty girl said, "You, too." Reluctantly, she shook Dad's hand.

The sun is in my eyes. The sun is in my eyes. How can I see with the sun in my eyes?

"I don't know," I say, to that gray vagueness where my interviewer was wont to reside. "I don't know, I just don't know. Maybe Mom and Dad and me, maybe the truth is we'd all grown apart just a little bit. Just a little too far apart, somehow."

FLASHBACK 15B

The kitchen of the Malibu house was very modern, in white Formica and stainless steel. At the butcher-block central island sat Hoskins, in his butler's tuxedo, obediently looking at photos being shown to him by Mom. Jack entered the room, unwary, then saw what was going on and tried to reverse his field and slide back on out of there. But it was too late; Mom had seen him. Looking up, waving a handful of photos at him, she said, "Come here, Sonny. Cousin Gertrude sent more pictures."

"That's nice," Jack said, from the doorway. "You and Hoskins—"

"I want *you* to see these pictures, Sonny," Mom insisted.

Reluctantly, Jack crossed the room, stood beside Hoskins, and looked down at the pictures.

"Here's Edwina on her sled," Mom said. "Cute?"

"Cute," said Jack.

"Here's Mabel's Doberman pinscher with its new collar on," Mom said. "Isn't that adorable?"

"Adorable," said Jack.

"Here's Mrs. Wallace's new refrigerator," Mom said.

"Mom," said Jack, "I don't even *know* Mrs. Wallace."

Suddenly furious, Mom turned hot, enraged eyes on Jack and snarled at him through gritted teeth: "You don't have to know Mrs. Wallace to look at her new *refrigerator*."

Jack nodded, his skin paler around the eyes. He bent his head to look at Mrs. Wallace's refrigerator.

My hand is in front of my eyes because of that sunlight, that sunlight pressing down on me, like looking up through water at the sky and seeing only white, the waves moving, the whiteness glaring on my eyeballs.

"Mr. Pine?"

"Yes yes yes," I say. "I'm all right. I'm here. I know what's going on. You are interviewing me. I am telling you my story. I am telling you about Mom and Dad, and how after a while Buddy and I decided maybe it would be better if we moved away from the beach for a while."

FLASHBACK 15C

The living room without its party, without the fire crackling cozily in the central fireplace, seemed larger and more impersonal. Moving through this space as though it were truly large, a vast desert, was a Guatemalan maid, slowly and ineptly dusting. Dust motes in the air followed her lazily from place to place.

Mom entered, in a vicious mood, clutching handfuls of snapshots. "Where's my Jack?" she demanded, glowering at the maid. "Where's my Sonny Boy?"

"Gone away," the maid told her.

"Gone away?" Mom glared so hard she looked as though she wanted to bite the maid's nose off. "Gone where?"

"Topanga Canyon," the maid said.

Mom blinked. She looked around. She said, "With Buddy? When's he coming back?"

"He no comin' back," the maid said.

Mom rose on the balls of her feet, red splotches appearing on her cheeks. "What? What the hell do you know?"

"They no comin' back," the maid repeated. All of the unfairness of her life was summed up in those words.

Mom squinted her eyes down to little slits and thrust her jaw at the maid. "Who *are* you, anyway?" she wanted to know.

The maid curtsied; dust motes ebbed and flowed all about her. "I am Constanza," she said. "I'm an illegal, so I gotta stay in the job."

Mom said, "You mean, Hoskins is gone, too?"

"Oh, sure," Constanza said. "He no illegal. He can quit any damn time. He say so."

"Dammit to hell and back," Mom said. "I wanted to show him these new pictures."

"Well, he gone," Constanza said, and sighed.

Mom studied the maid, then thrust photos at her, saying, "Here, *you* can look at them." Shoving a picture into Constanza's hands, she said, "This is the twins with their rock polisher. Don't they look alike? Bet you can't tell which one is Bobby."

Constanza dropped her dust rag on a chair and considered the photo. She pointed. "That one," she said.

Impressed, Mom said, "Pretty good! Come on, sit down here. Let's take a look at these."

Mom and the Guatemalan maid sat side by side on a sofa that faced the sea. They did not look out. They bent their heads together over the pictures, one by one.

All this light, this light, this glaring light. I can't even look up anymore. I have to talk to my interviewer's gray shins. I sit tailor-fashion, legs folded in front of me, knees rising winglike on both sides. I lean forward over this nest of legs, and I pull my brows down low over my eyes because of all that sunlight, and I tell my interviewer's shins, "Mom and Dad were happy there at the beach. It wouldn't have been fair to take them away to the ranch."

"Did they ever see the ranch at all?"

"Oh, no. I didn't see any point in confusing them." I touch my fingers to my forehead, and something is cold. Which is it that's cold? Is it my fingers, or is it my forehead? Shouldn't a person *know* these things? Shouldn't a person *be able to tell* these things about his own fucking body?

I am atremble with rage. I can feel it. I know it's bad for me. I am not supposed to feel great emotions, not the large emotions; they are all very bad for me. I can *perform* them, none better, but I am not supposed to *experience* them.

I take a deep breath, full of splinters and broken glass. I exhale dark, foul, noxious vapors. My hand (possibly cold) moves down from my forehead (possibly cold) to my lap (oh, most definitely cold).

"The ranch," my interviewer says.

"The ranch. Yes. The ranch was good for me then. I found peace." I lift my head, ignoring the harsh glare, my own face gleaming and shining. I smile, my light brighter than the sun. "I also found God," I say.

FLASHBACK 16

It's wild, rough country, Topanga Canyon, tumbled and brown, its high-shouldered hills brushed with lacy pine, deep damp crevasses choked with ferns. The canyon is many canyons, snaking and slicing and filigreeing through the hills. The two-lane twisty road climbs up from the sea at Malibu, north and east into the dusty hills lying just next door to Los Angeles but on the map of time a millennium away.

The people of Topanga Canyon are loners, oddballs, dropouts, believers in alternatives. They are not fierce pioneers, the progenitors of capitalists, but gentle solitaries, aware of the fragility of all things in the fragility of themselves. They do not pound deep foundations into the earth's skin, do not thrust steel erections at the indifferent sky. Their houses are modest, set apart from one another, colored in earth tones of orange and brown and green. Unpainted rail fences enclose their horses: yes, they have horses. Their driveways are likelier to be of gravel or dirt than glittering blacktop. They grow eggplant and tomatoes and marijuana. Their lives are so in tune with their environment, they blend in so well with their terrain, that they are barely noticeable in their bivouacs up the steep sides of the many canyon walls. Only their television reception dishes stand out, amazingly, looking in this setting like UFOs from outer space. (They believe in UFOs.)

The horse Jack rode up the firm tan trail from his house toward the peak of the hill was a frisky roan, high-stepping, flaring its eyes and chewing its bit as though auditioning for a portrait with Napoleon. The man and horse following just behind him up the trail were both of a very different order, the horse being a placid and thick-bodied speckled gray, its rider a comfortable and stocky and prosperous-looking man of fifty-something in a minister's black suit and white collar. He was hatless, his thinning gray hair disordered from its usual wavy exacti-tude.

Jack reined to a stop at the crest of the hill. Broken land stretched out before him, with very few signs of human habitation. Behind them, down the hill, was Jack's own ranch house, a low structure of dull red brick with wood-shingled roof, blending into its location, watched over by sentinels of tall pine.

When the second man reined in beside him, Jack turned on him a face lit with a beatific smile. Gesturing broadly, he said, "Isn't this great, Reverend Cornbraker?"

Rev. Elwood Cornbraker nodded slowly in judicious agreement, accepting the compliment to God's landscap-ing on God's behalf. "It is truly magnificent, John," he said, and gentled his gentle horse with a pat on the side of its neck.

Jack half stood in the saddle, raising his arms upward toward the empyrean, gazing out at the wild and tumbled land. "What a place for a temple!" he cried. "Reverend, we could buy some of that land over there next to mine, that ridge there with the yellow flowers on it—"

Reverend Cornbraker quietly but firmly interrupted, with a friendly and forgiving smile, saying, "God's true temple is in our hearts, John."

Humble, dropping back down onto the saddle, folding his hands on the pommel and turning to bow his head toward the reverend, Jack said, "Oh, I know that, Reverend Cornbraker. You've made me understand so much that I didn't understand before."

The reverend made a small gesture of his right hand, as though he were giving absolution. "I know you mean well, John," he said, "but we don't need to erect a temple to our Maker here in Topanga Canyon. The testimony of our lives is the true manner of our attracting His attention. Our little chapel over in Pasadena is, I'm sure, good enough for God. Modest enough for God."

"Oh, that's a wonderful chapel, Reverend," Jack told him, with fervent conviction. "That's a *cathedral*."

Modestly, Reverend Cornbraker permitted a pleased smile to crease his well-fed features. "God and I thank you, John," he said. "You needn't spend your life's earnings on temples. God doesn't need that from you. All you must do is continue to tithe to the church."

"Oh, *sure*, Reverend," Jack said. "You know I'll do that. In fact, I've got a check for you right now back at the ranch. Ten percent of a salary payment that just came in. I've got it all set and waiting for you."

But the reverend didn't need such reassurances. He gracefully waved that away, then had to gentle his horse once more as he said, "That's fine, John. Just fine. God thanks you for your faith and confidence in Him."

"And the commercial I shot? How's that doing?"

The reverend smiled in such a way as to show that he disapproved of the terminology but would not make a point of it. Having made that point, he said, "The television message you were so good as to film for us has been very . . . productive."

"I'm glad," Jack said. He sat atop his spirited mount, gazing away at the hills and canyons that were already God's temple. "It's good to be alive!" he cried, and the landscape gave the echo back.

"Yes, it is, John," the Reverend Cornbraker said.

I can *see* with my forehead.

Is this a new thing? Does this exist in the annals of science? Am I the first of a new breed?

I can see with my forehead. The glare became so bright, the sheen of the sun so fierce, that now I've closed my eyes, and still I can see all that light, bright white light, see it beating on my forehead, ramming its way through the skull and into my brain. I am *seeing* the light. With my forehead.

Which of my doctors could I tell this to? One that won't steal the credit, of course. I want this phenomenon named for *me*, doc, not for you.

"Mr. Pine?"

Oh. *Him*. My forehead sees him, a dark gray lump at two o'clock high; my interviewer. "I'm here," I promise him.

"You were telling me about the Rev. Elwood Cornbraker."

"Ah, yes." My eyes open briefly, but that's an error; I snap them shut again. I'll keep watch with my forehead. "Life was good with Reverend Cornbraker, good and full and sweet. All at once there was purpose to my existence. I gave him a tenth of my income; that's tithing. That wasn't much, was it? After agents, managers, alimony, child support, attorneys, accountants, taxes, that left me a good three or four percent of my income for myself to spend any way I pleased. That's not such a bad deal, is it? Is it?"

"I guess not," the interviewer says, but I can hear in his voice he's not so sure.

"Well, *I* didn't think it was a bad deal," I say. "I was happy with the reverend. I was at peace with myself. All my nightmares went away, my old guilts—"

"Which old guilts, Mr. Pine?"

"—just seemed to disappear. I was washed clean, in the blood of the Lamb."

"Which old guilts were those, Mr. Pine?"

Persistent son of a bitch. What kind of fucking deferential interviewer *is* this anyway? Why don't I just tell him to go shove his ball-point up his ass and get out of here, the interview's over? Why don't I just—

No. Not a good idea to make the press suspicious. You never know what they'll come up with.

"Which particular old guilts were you talking about, Mr. Pine?"

My forehead gives him a crafty look. "*All* my old guilts," I tell him. "They just faded away. For a little while, I was at peace with myself. I was content. It was such a strange feeling, that. But good. I'd been working too hard, piling up the money, the pictures, the credits, working in three bad pictures for every good one, and Reverend Cornbraker was the one who told me I didn't have to do that. He's the one who told me working compulsively like that was a way of running away from something that scared me, but that I didn't have to be scared anymore. I could take my time."

"And did you?"

"Most of my people didn't like it." My forehead smiles, remembering. (My forehead can smile, too, and frown if necessary.) "Agents," I say. "Managers. Even Buddy. They all *liked* me working, it meant more money for everybody. Reverend Cornbraker was the one who gave me permission to slow down, and I did, and then it lasted just a little while."

"And then it came to an end."

My forehead gives him a rueful look. "Sure did. I know Buddy meant well with what he did, but sometimes, even now, I find myself wishing I'd never learned the truth."

FLASHBACK 16A

The living room of the ranch stretched across the entire front of the place so that in three directions, through the six-over-six windows flanked by red and white check curtains, the views were of wild and tumbled hills, tall pines, thick untamed underbrush, and high triangles of pale blue sky. Not one artifact of man was visible out there, as though the ranch were a trapper's cabin high in the Rockies in a silent movie. Except in color, of course.

Within, the ambiance was of a trapper who'd done very well for himself; an Astor, perhaps. The knotty-pine furniture with rosy chintz-covered cushions was rustic but comfortable. The Indian rugs on the floor were muted Mondrians, schematic, symmetric, each with its tiny deliberate unnoticeable imperfection, placed there so the gods—who think of perfection as their own prerogative—would not become jealous and take vengeance on the carpet's maker. Or owner.

Balancing the broad, heavy, dark-wood front door, on the opposite wall, was a huge fieldstone fireplace in which a construct of large logs slowly burned, orange and red. Above the fireplace, where the moose's head might be expected—and where, until recently, the moose's head had in fact been displayed—a wide amber painting hung, called "The Return from Calvary": the weeping women in the foreground, the dirt road curving back and up to Golgotha, the three crosses tiny but prominent there against the cloud-raging sky.

A sound of Gregorian chants filled the clean air of the high-ceilinged room. Jack, dressed in red floral neckerchief, checked flannel shirt, Levis, and well-worn cowboy boots, sat in a wide knotty-pine armchair near the fire and read a copy of *Lives of the Saints*. Peace, that peace that surpasseth understanding, abided in the room.

Hoskins, dressed quite similarly in style to Jack, although his neckerchief was blue and his cowboy boots less worn, and the entire sartorial approach less suited to his size, shape, age, and demeanor, entered bearing a silver tray on which stood an opened can of Coke and an ice-cube-filled glass. He placed the can and the glass on the rough-legged knotty-pine table beside Jack's chair.

"Thank you, Hoskins," Jack said, glancing up from his book. "We're all equal in the eyes of God, you know."

Hoskins bowed from the waist and from the neck. "And very good of Him it is, too, sir," he said.

Jack returned to his reading. Hoskins bowed again and departed toward the rear of the house, carrying the silver tray. Jack poured some Coke into the glass, waited for the bubbles to subside, and sipped. He returned to his reading.

The Coke was not quite finished and the ice cubes not quite half their original size twenty minutes later when the broad front door opened and Buddy entered, also dressed in the same style as Jack, except that his neckerchief was black and his boots were a highly polished snakeskin. In this setting, dressed in such similar fashion, that old resemblance of their youth was more pronounced again, as though they were cousins employed by the same rancher.

Jack looked up, as always pleased to see his friend. "What say, Buddy? Have a good trip to town?"

"In a way," Buddy said. He was carrying a large manila envelope in his left hand. He shut the front door behind him, crossed the room, and sat in the chair on the other side of the small table bearing the Coke. Jack went back to his reading, and Buddy sat watching him, his expression troubled. He fidgeted with the manila envelope in his hands. One Gregorian chant sighed and reverberated to an end, and a moment later another one started.

Jack looked up, mildly interested. "Something wrong, Buddy?"

"I'm sorry, Dad," Buddy said, looking and sounding sorry, "but I've got some bad news."

"There is no bad news in the eyes of the Lord, Buddy," Jack reminded him. "Just good news."

Buddy took a deep breath, and then blurted out: "The Reverend Elwood Cornbraker's a phony."

Smiling, confident, Jack shook his head. A finger marked his place in *Lives of the Saints*. He said, "Oh, no, he isn't, Buddy."

"But he is."

"Buddy," Jack said, "I know you haven't felt the call as strongly as I have, but you can be sure of one thing: Reverend Cornbraker's as real as God Himself."

Buddy looked grim. He said, "His real name's Ralph Hatch. He's done time twice in federal pens on mail fraud."

Still confident, Jack smiled in commiseration and said, "Not possible, Buddy. Mistaken identification. Goodness just shines from the reverend's brow."

Buddy said, "He also did a couple years in Indiana State Penitentiary for child molestation. He liked to take pictures of himself with the kids."

Buddy tossed the manila envelope into Jack's lap, atop the copy of *Lives of the Saints* he held there. Jack stared at it, his expression growing more and more blank. Finally, with nothing showing on his face at all, he withdrew his finger from *Lives of the Saints*, placed the book next to the

119

Coke can on the table, and picked up the envelope. Even with nothing showing on his face, it was clear from the slope of his shoulders and the slowness of his movements that he really and truly didn't want to know what was inside that envelope. He opened its flap, then looked across at Buddy, but there was no reprieve there. Buddy sat and waited and watched.

Jack sighed. He slid two fingers down into the manila envelope and partially brought out an eight-by-ten glossy photograph. He turned envelope and photograph around so he could look at the picture, then sat for a long silent moment unmoving, studying what he saw.

Buddy cleared his throat. He said, "The Feds got a tip that Hatch was back in business."

Jack glanced at Buddy. "A tip? Who from?"

"Anonymous," Buddy said. "I figure we'll never know who blew the whistle."

Jack looked at his friend. He nodded. He looked again at the photograph.

Buddy said, "Hatch is under surveillance now; they'll close in soon when they've got all the evidence they need. I didn't want you to be there when it happened."

Still looking at the photo, Jack said, "Turn off that fucking music, will you, Buddy?"

Buddy got to his feet and crossed the room to where the stereo equipment was concealed in an old marble-topped dry sink. While he hunkered in front of it, opening its door, Jack removed three more large photos from the envelope, dropped the envelope on the floor, and looked at the pictures, turning them this way and that.

The Gregorian chant stopped. Buddy rose, shut the dry sink's doors, and came back across the room to sit once more at Jack's left hand.

His manner calm, judicious, Jack tapped the photo he was looking at and said, "I didn't know anybody could do it in that position."

Buddy leaned forward over the Coke can. Jack turned the picture so they could both look at it. Buddy said, "It's young bones. They're supple."

"Try that with a grown-up," Jack suggested, "you'd break something."

"I'm sorry, Dad," Buddy said somberly. He kept looking at the photograph.

Jack also kept looking at the photograph. "Nothing to be sorry about, Buddy. I appreciate what you've done. It's better to know."

Jack studied the photographs. Buddy studied Jack, waiting it out.

LUDE

O'Connor looks at Jack Pine's closed eyes. They've been closed for some time, down beneath his palely gleaming forehead. When they first went to half-mast, and then all the way shut, O'Connor was worried, expecting the actor to pass out again, but in some ways he's been more coherent since the hatches were battened, speaking with a kind of pathetic vivacity about his religious period, moving right along in sensible sentences, almost totally free of non sequitur and silence.

Until now. A silence has now arrived and is lengthening. O'Connor wants the star to tell the story himself, all the irrelevant stuff just as much as the stuff that has a bearing on the case, so he's been giving the fellow his head, letting him ramble on. But silence doesn't help, doesn't explain what happened here last night. At last, O'Connor leans forward, softly says, "Mr. Pine? You're at the ranch. The Reverend Cornbraker is a fake."

A long low sigh escapes the actor's lips. In equal and opposite reaction, he settles back and to the left, listing slightly, like a ship suffering a small hole below the water line.

"Mr. Pine?"

His voice slurring, sleepy, hoarse, Jack murmurs, "I was happy, then . . . on the ranch . . . with God." And he folds over and down onto the slate, on his left side, curled into fetal position.

"Shit!" O'Connor says, and looks around, wishing there was somebody else to take over this duty. It's like pulling teeth, for Christ's sake. "Mr. Pine?" he says, then louder, calling, "Mr. Pine? Mr. Pine?"

No reaction. The actor's breathing seems shallower, more ragged. His forehead seems even paler and gleams less. Beginning to feel concern, O'Connor looks toward the house, calling, "Hoskins!"

And that faithful servant appears at once, moving at an ungainly but rapid trot from the house, holding up in one hand a hypodermic needle. When he arrives, he nods at O'Connor. "You called," he says.

"You see," O'Connor says, gesturing at the unconscious actor.

"Yes," Hoskins says, nodding. "I thought it might be time for dire measures."

Dropping to one knee beside his recumbent employer, Hoskins deftly pulls up the unconscious man's pale blue terry-cloth robe, revealing a buttock as high and round and pale and vulnerable as that sleeping forehead. With practiced economy, Hoskins jabs the hypodermic needle into that buttock.

"George!" exclaims Jack, in his sleep, in playful mock surprise, as his limbs quiver and are still.

Steadily, Hoskins depresses the plunger. Steadily, the clear fluid in the syringe flows into Jack Pine's bum. Withdrawing the needle, Hoskins restores the robe to its former position and rises, saying, "He'll be right as rain in no time now, sir."

"For how long?" O'Connor asks. The pages of notes inexorably filling his notebook seem—at least at this stage—mostly useless, with no more than hints and faint clues as to what led to the dreadful finish last night in this house. Nevertheless, this still seems to O'Connor the best way to get at the truth, unless it's going to take forever. "How long can I have him?" O'Connor asks. "How long can he operate at all?"

"Hard to say," Hoskins says, studying the fallen actor. He shrugs, his manner brisk. "Call when needed," he suggests, and strides away again toward the house, empty syringe held high.

O'Connor, remaining in his canvas chair, leans toward the unconscious man. Was that movement just now, or merely the play of light and shadow as a small cloud crossed the sun? "Mr. Pine?" O'Connor calls. "Mr. Pine?"

"I left my homework on the bus," comes the murmured answer.

"Mr. Pine! Dammit, wake up!"

Jack Pine twitches, all over his body, then rolls out flat onto his back, eyes wide open, staring upward, drawing the pale ashiness of the summer sky deep into those eyes, so that they seem ancient and blind, consumed with gray fire. "It all goes back," he croaks, in a voice that echoes as though emerging from the deepest pit of Hell, "it all goes back—I remember—"

Screams, screaming, engine roars, flashing lights in red and white reflecting from the bumper chrome, slicking on the heaving trunk of the car, madness, danger, movement, peril, speed . . .

· · ·

"No!"

I roll over onto my face, nose rooting deep into the cool hard slate; pain is good, it distracts, it drives the thoughts away. Reaching down and back behind myself, I grab handfuls of terry-cloth robe, pull it up over my head, hiding from the sky and the past and everything. Cool air soothes my bare behind, where one spot tickles and stings; a mosquito must have got me while I was napping. (Good, an irrelevant thought. Keep 'em coming, for Christ's sake!)

"Mr. Pine? Mr. Pine?"

I thrash with my ankles in protest, wanting no one to be here, wanting to be called from nowhere, wanting oblivion, dear sweet oblivion, dear God *oblivion*.

"It's me, Mr. Pine," the maddening voice says. "Michael O'Connor."

I stop kicking with my ankles, stop stubbing my toes against the patio slate. I lift my head, wearing the terry-cloth robe around my face like a pale blue monk's cowl. I gaze away across my gray-green lawn beneath the gray-blue sky, past my gray-white house. I become thoughtful. "Michael O'Connor," I say, judiciously, hefting the name, contemplating it. "A good name," I decide. "Very solid. *I'd* like to be Michael O'Connor for a while. Several days. Drive a Volvo." I twist around to look past my pale blue cowl and my pale blue shoulder and my pale white ass at this person named Michael O'Connor, whoever or what-ever else he might be. I see a neat dull man, nondescript, and yet somehow familiar. Am I going to be expected to *remember* something? Ignoring that idea, I say, "Do you drive a Volvo?"

"As a matter of fact," he said, "no. A Saab."

"Damn," I say. "Wrong again." Then I become more aware of that gleaming ass of mine, down there beyond my blue shoulder. I'm *naked* in front of this guy! A wind must have come up, blown my robe up over me while I was deep in contemplation of, of, of something or other.

I pull the robe back down over myself, roll over, con-tinue the robe adjustments for some little while, and at last sit up, barely even noticing how easy it *is* to sit up. I must be in better shape than I thought. I look at Michael O'Connor, a neat and self-contained man, if drab, seated with knees together, pen in right hand, some sort of memo pad on his lap. He looks familiar, in a kind of a way. Memory stirs. (Not *that* memory. *This* memory.) I say, "Aren't you the guy I was talking to the other day?"

"Just now," O'Connor tells me. "Right here. We've been talking right here."

"I thought you were the guy," I say, smiling with easy familiarity, covering a certain embarrassment. "Remind me," I say, "fill me in. Insurance?"

"Actually," O'Connor says, with a charming diffidence, "I wanted to know about Buddy Pal. You were telling me your life story."

Then it comes rushing back. (*That* doesn't. *This* does.) I slap my forehead, I wave my arms around, I kick my legs, I do every silent-movie how-dumb-I-am move I can re-member. I say, "The interview! Of course!" Then, confidentially, man to man, bringing him aboard, making him a member of the team, I say, "Pal, you gotta forgive me on this. My schedule's very complex. I'm just off a picture, you know, the *Gone with the Wind* remake, and I just . . ." I wave hands.

"I understand," O'Connor says. Sympathetic guy. I could get along with this fella.

I open my heart to him even more. "I was straight for weeks, Mike, and then—Is it Mike or Michael?"

"Usually Michael," he says.

I might have guessed. There's something prissy about this guy, uptight, not loose and relaxed. Well, anyway, let's befriend him just the same. "I was straight a long time, Michael," I say, "and then something happened, upset me, I fell— . . ."

"What was that, Mr. Pine? What upset you?"

"Doesn't matter, Michael," I tell him, waving it away with a carefree hand. "That's ancient history. That's archives, Michael. The point is, I *wasted* myself. I'd been taking a taste here, a hit there, a pop somewhere else, you know what I mean? Maintaining. That's my idea of being on the dope wagon, Michael, maintaining that nice balance, that easy lope through life." And I wonder, am I using his name too often? Do I risk moving beyond manly camaraderie to starrish condescension? Best back off; keep on the good side of the press, that's the name of the game. "Where were we?" I ask him. "Did I tell you about Marcia, my first wife?"

"Yes, sir," he says.

"Pow!" I tell him, taking a poke at the air. "Right in the kisser, you know?"

"You were at the ranch," he reminds me. "Buddy Pal had just told you the Reverend Cornbraker was a con man."

"And child molester," I say. "Oh, yeah. Things got kind of grim at the ranch around then. Meantime, life wasn't so hot down at the beach, either."

FLASHBACK 15D

The kitchen of the Malibu house was as modern and shiny as ever, still a pale symphony in white and stainless steel and blond butcher block, but there was an indefinable sense of laxity about the place now, an impression of disinterest, a falling-off of care. On the shelf beneath the cabinets, for instance, the canisters were no longer in size places. Some silverware lay about, the trash can was full, and the pot on a back burner of the stove had a faintly grungy look.

Dad had brought a small portable television set into the kitchen and put it on the white table at the eat-in end of the room. He sat there now, switching his teeth from hand to hand as he watched golf. At the butcher-block island, Constanza sat on a high stool, looking at snapshots and drinking a glass of milk, with the milk carton near at hand. Over by the refrigerator (fingermarks around the handle), Mom was angrily on the phone, saying, "Whadaya mean, he isn't there? You *always* say he isn't there! He's my son, isn't he? He's my own goddamn son out of my own goddamn *body*, isn't he? Why can't I talk to my own goddamn son if I want to"

"The twins are gettin' bigger," Constanza said, riffling slowly through the snapshots.

Mom bared her teeth at the phone. "You're a lying sack of shit!" she yelled. "That's what you are!" She slammed the phone onto its hook, veering away, her hand clutching at air, her mouth snapping like a piranha. "He can't do that to me!" she cried, and glared across the table at Constanza, who looked warily back at her, beginning to sense that things were going radically wrong. "Why do I have to put up with this?" Mom demanded.

"I no know," Constanza said, trying to come up with a soft answer in an unfamiliar language.

"How can he treat me this way?" Mom yelled, and waved her hand, crying, "Give me that milk!"

Bewildered, Constanza handed across the butcher block to Mom her half-finished glass of milk. Mom grabbed it, lifted it, and poured it on her own head. Milk streamed down over her face and ran into her tight gray hair. She flung the glass away; it bounced off a cabinet and smashed on the floor. Ignoring the noise, Mom lunged forward as though somebody else were trying to beat her to it and grabbed up the plastic carton of milk. It was about a third full.

Constanza, wide-eyed, shaking, scrambled clumsily off the stool and backed away from the butcher block, as Mom upended the milk carton over her head, milk splashing down onto her head, dripping off her nose, staining the shoulders of her old gray cardigan, gluing her hair to her scalp. Flinging the empty carton away, Mom glared at Constanza and moved around the butcher block after her. Constanza moved, too, keeping the bulk of the butcher-block island between them, and slowly they reversed their original positions.

Mom stopped; so did Constanza. Trying to look sly, but still looking mostly enraged and out of control, Mom said, "We got any more milk?"

"I no know," quavered Constanza.

"You're lying, you dirty wetback!" Mom yelled, and

waved both arms around. "Look in that refrigerator, and you'd better come up with something!"

Shaking with fear, Constanza stumbled to the refrigerator, managed on the second try to get it open, and brought out two full cartons of milk, which she set on the butcher block as though they were offerings to a violent god.

"Open them!"

The refrigerator door snicked itself shut behind Constanza as she fumbled open first one and then the other carton. Mom grabbed them, one at a time, poured out great gushing white streams of milk onto her head, drenching herself, sopping her old print dress, getting milk even into her shoes.

Over by the television set, Dad snickered but didn't look away from the golf game. "Pouring milk on her head again," he told himself.

Mom flung the first carton away, and then the second, and they bounced and rolled around the room. Pointing past Constanza at the refrigerator, she yelled, "Give me that half-and-half! I saw that half-and-half in there!"

Constanza nodded spastically, backing away from Mom toward the refrigerator, not willing to look away from the older woman, but having to in order to open the refrigerator door, search the interior, bring out the nearly full small carton of half-and-half. On the other side of the room, Dad nodded his head in satisfaction, clucking the teeth in his hands.

The half-and-half poured more slowly through Mom's matted hair, down around her ears, through her eyebrows, and over her hot mad eyes. She hurled the empty carton back over her shoulder, away, away, anywhere. It barely missed Dad, who didn't even blink.

Mom took a deep breath, fists clenched, knuckles standing out against the thin white milk-stained flesh. "Heavy cream!" she screamed. "Give me heavy cream! I want heavy creeeeaaammmmmmm!"

I rock back and forth on my stinging rump, the heels of my hands pressed to my stinging eyes. Oh, this just came over me, this just came over me, I must regain control.

I regain control. I stop rocking back and forth. I lower my hands from my calm face. I say, "Finally, I just had to go down there to the beach house myself."

FLASHBACK 15E

Jack, in Hush Puppies and chinos and polo shirt, paced back and forth on the gray board deck of the Malibu house. Through the glass doors of the living room, Dad could be seen watching a bicycle race on television. Out of the curtained glass doors of the bedroom came Mom, soaking wet, furious, a crushed empty milk carton in her hand. She stomped across the deck toward Jack, her shoes making squelching sounds. "So there he is," she snarled. "The big man."

"Mom," Jack said helplessly, spreading his hands. "What do you *want* from me?"

"Airline tickets," Mom snapped.

Startled, not having expected this at all, Jack said, "What? Where to?"

"Home, of course." Mom gave the house a look of hate, gave the Pacific Ocean a look of hate, gave Jack a look of hate. She said, "What is this cruddy place to Dad and me? Nothing but sand and faggots everywhere. We want to go home to Grover's Corners, where we belong."

"Mom!" Jack cried, stricken. "You can't mean that! You can't leave me!"

"The hell I can't," Mom told him. "And I'll knock you down if you get in my way."

Bitter, betrayed, deeply hurt, Jack raised himself to his full height and spoke with slow, mature grief. He said, "You don't love me. You *never* loved me. You never loved *anybody*. You don't know *how* to love."

With impatient asperity, Mom said, "Well, who ever said I did? I never wanted children in the first place. It was all your father's fault. He could never do anything right his whole entire life long. Though I do have to admit he was right when it came to this."

"When it came to what?" Jack asked.

"You," Mom told him. "We didn't have children, we had *you*. Mewling and puking, whining about yourself from the day you were born. A weakling and a coward. You'll never amount to *anything*."

"But—" Jack stared at her, not knowing where to start. "I make millions!" he cried. "I'm rich and famous! They write me up in magazines!" Madly, wildly gesturing at the house, he cried, "Look what I bought you!"

"You'll never buy *me*, Sunny Jim," Mom said. She threw the empty milk carton at his feet, spun about, and marched back into the house.

Jack, devastated, slowly sank to his knees, staring through the glass doors into the house. On his knees, he kept going, curving slowly in over his stomach, his torso bending downward until his forehead touched the warm wood of the deck. He stayed in that position, hands folded over stomach, forehead and knees and toes touching the deck. A faint moaning sound came from him.

A faint moaning sound comes from me. I close my mouth over it, and when that doesn't work I close my throat. This time, that's all it takes. (Sometimes, I have to close my hands around my throat and squeeze real tight to make it stop. I'm glad I don't have to do that in front of Michael O'Connor, intrepid reporter.)

Calm again, I say, "Well, I felt I had to go along with Mom's wishes."

Sympathy in his voice, O'Connor says, "She was a little rough on you, wasn't she?"

"We all have our needs," I assure him, feeling how placid I am, how easy in my mind. "I bought those airline tickets for Mom and Dad and said good-bye. Buddy drove them to the airport. All that was left was to have Constanza stop the milk deliveries, and it was as though the whole episode had never been."

"But—" O'Connor says. "You wanted them there. That was the whole point, wasn't it?"

"Their needs were different from mine," I say, smiling

and smiling. "Besides, it all worked itself out, finally. It meant the house at the beach was available soon after that when I needed it."

"Needed it?"

"Yes." Remembered sunshine floods my eyes. "Just around that time, you see," I say, "I fell in love again."

FLASHBACK 17

The living room of the beach house looked much as it had before, except that now the walls were completely lined with bookcases filled with heavy serious tomes. These bookcases caused the furniture to be moved inward, cutting down on party space, making the room cozier but less open. The television set was gone. The fire in the central white-brick fireplace was the same as before, a neat construct of large logs, burning slowly with lovely dancing flames in orange and red that gave more beauty than heat.

Lorraine Morriswood entered the room. A tall, slender, beautiful, brainy young woman in tailored tweeds and dark-rimmed glasses, Lorraine moved with a kind of horsy assurance that was simultaneously elegant and very erotic. She circled the room, obviously looking for something, and just as obviously not finding it. Finally she stopped, raised her head, and called, "Darling?"

From somewhere else in the house, Jack's voice answered, calling, "Yes, darling?"

"Darling," called Lorraine, "where's Kierkegaard?"

Jack strolled into the room, wearing black loafers, dark slacks, tweed jacket with leather elbow patches, and a paisley ascot. "Gosh, darling," he said, "I haven't seen it."

Pointing to a nearby end table, Lorraine said, "I'm sure, darling, I left it right there."

Jack looked around, then snapped his fingers and said, "*I* know, darling. I bet Constanza put it away when she was in here cleaning."

Lorraine turned in a slow ironic circle, on her face an expression of mock despair as she gazed helplessly at all the bookcases. "Oh, dear, darling," she said. "And Constanza's hopeless when it comes to the alphabet. Lord knows where poor old Keirkegaard's got to."

Jack, with a merry laugh, took her by the elbow, stopping her steady circling motion, turning her toward him. "I tell you what, darling," he said. "Let's let poor old Kierkegaard just go hang for a while."

"Why, darling," Lorraine said, with an arch look, "whatever can you mean?"

"You *know*, darling," Jack told her, and his hand stroked slowly up and down her arm.

She laughed, a rich throaty sound, her head thrown back. Removing her glasses, she dropped them on the table from which Kierkegaard had disappeared, then reached up and back to remove the barrettes holding her rich full hair. Auburn waves shook loose, framing her face, reflecting deep reds from the fireplace. She threw her long arms around Jack, and passionately they embraced. Laughing, kissing, fondling, licking, murmuring, stripping the clothes away from each other, they descended toward the fur rug stretched before the fire. A warm musk filled the air. . . .

There. See? There *are* happy memories. In isolation, there are moments in one's history one can look back upon with pleasure, saying to oneself, of oneself, *"Then* it was good to be alive."

I smile at Michael, who will never in his drab life know even *one* moment like those evenings in front of the fire with sweet Lorraine. "This is how we met," I say. "Lorraine Morriswood was doing her doctoral thesis at Chicago on Post-Camp Male Nonaggression in the Popular Arts. Naturally, I was one of the people she had to interview."

"Sure," O'Connor says. "Makes sense."

"Just like you're interviewing me now, Michael," I say. "Only, that time it led to greater things."

"She was your second wife," O'Connor says. The brilliant researcher struts his stuff again.

"That's right," I agree. "Lorraine and I sensed right away we were meant for each other. It was a whirlwind romance, taking us both out of our mundane concerns, our everyday affairs."

"I guess you figured you were due for some happiness right around then," O'Connor says.

"Very good, Michael," I say, smiling upon him, pleased to find in him this unexpected capacity for the dramatic *mot*. I may even read the piece he writes on me. "Anyway," I say, "we had, Lorraine and I had, a small private wedding at the London Registry Office."

"I remember," O'Connor says, "the news footage of the two of you coming out of there, protected by the bobbies, with the big crowd of fans in the street."

"They're there all the time," I say modestly. "I believe they camp out there. Some say they've been there since the Paul McCartney wedding, others that it goes back as far as Elizabeth Taylor. Some scholars suggest a Druid connection, but I myself don't go that far. In any event, as you may have surmised, Lorraine introduced me to a world I'd never known, a world of the mind. Through Lorraine, I met some of the foremost thinkers of our time, men and women who could understand a universe in a grain of sand. And Lorraine . . . Lorraine understood me more deeply and truly than anyone ever before, or since."

FLASHBACK 17A

The beach along here, in the fog, was empty, untouched, timeless. It wasn't even possible to guess the time of day, except to know that it *was* day, the sun far off somewhere creating a luminous pearlescence in the haze, so that every drop of suspended moisture in the air was distinct and separate, another silver-gray perfect beryl. In this gauzy light, the broad tan beach was as clean as the evening of the first day of creation, while the modestly murmuring sea was a textured charcoal gray with highlights in streaks of white, lapping along the shore. Visibility was down to perhaps eight or ten feet, so it was possible to think of oneself as being alone on the planet; or not even a planet, but some small asteroid, far from the trials of life.

Jack and his Lorraine came striding easily through the luminous fog, dressed in similar laced boots and baggy corduroy slacks and windbreakers with the hoods up around their faces. They walked hand in hand, and the fog condensed on their cheeks, sparkling there. "Gosh, darling," Jack said, "it's almost as though it's the beginning of the world, as though we're the first humans ever. Do you suppose we'd make the same sort of mistakes?"

Laughing at him with friendly familiarity, Lorraine said, "But, darling, how could you be the first man? You're so much closer to the last."

Jack's smile grew blank. "I don't think I follow, darling," he said.

Lorraine shook her head, lovingly amused. "You know," she said, "it's fascinating sometimes to see how unaware you remain of your symbolic relationship with the mass audience."

"Unaware?" Jack asked. "Do you think so?"

"Yes, of course, darling," Lorraine told him. "Do you have any idea who you really are?"

"I'm a movie star, darling."

"Yes, but why *you*?" Lorraine asked him. "Why do millions of people spend money to see *you* in the movies?"

"Gosh, darling," Jack said, open-eyed and clear-browed, "I don't know."

"You are, of course, wonderfully talented, darling," Lorraine said, "but honestly, you know, so are others. From the pool of talent in the world, the mass audience always chooses that one person, that tiny group of individuals, who represent the ethos of the age, its quintessence, its spirit and vitals. *You* are of that band, darling. Your talent launched you, but now it's the age itself that drives you. Another pilot is at the wheel. You are no longer under your own control."

"Sounds almost frightening," Jack said, with a light but respectful laugh.

"The symbolic freight you carry, darling," Lorraine assured him, "would crush a lesser man."

Pleased, smiling like a puppy, Jack said, "Do you really think so, darling?"

"Darling," Lorraine said, holding tightly to his hand as they strode along the beach, "in many ways you're a monster, a statement of infantile voracious appetite. And yet at the same time you are God's holy fool, the sacred monster, the innocent untouched by the harshness of

141

reality. You can be the hero, incredibly strong, and yet even I don't know the depths of your vulnerability."

Jack loved to hear talk about himself. He listened as they walked together, nodding, absorbed in what she was saying. "Tell me more," he said.

Lorraine was willing. "And yet, darling," she said, "in some ways you can represent evil as well. The innocent and the slayer of innocence all commingled together in one powerfully attractive package. And yet, how lightly you bear this burden."

With a brave laugh, looking at his Lorraine, Jack said, "Gosh, darling!"

The two walked on, along the beach, beside the whispering ocean, into the fog.

"**N**ever had I known any-
one so interested in *me*." I smile in contented reverie at my
interlocutor. "Do you know what I mean, Michael?" I am
remembering his name, even that. I am under control, by
God, I am the captain of my fucking fate, I am the master
of whatchamacallit. I say, "I don't mean *interested*, you
know? I mean . . . *interested!* You know?"

"I think I do," he says, gazing at me over his knees and
his notebook and his pencil and his nothing nose.

"I mean," I explain further, *"you're* interested in me,
right?"

"Yes, I am," he says.

"Your readers are interested in me," I say. "People going
to the movies are interested in me. *Everybody's* interested
in me. But not like Lorraine. She really dug down in there.
She really wanted to *know* me. But thank God she didn't
care about the details, you see what I mean?"

He frowns. "No," he says simply.

"Lorraine wasn't interested in my *biography*," I tell
Michael O'Connor. "She was interested in my *meaning*. My

biography is trash, don't you think I know that? Pop paperback history, a million pretentious movies, the same elements over and over again. The religious interlude, the failed *rapprochement* with the parents, the ghastly secret in the past, the casting couch, the betrayals, the glitzy locations, the glamorous diseased marriages, the problems with mood enhancers, the whole shmear. Lorraine didn't care about any of that. Her interest in me went deeper, into *why* these images are so powerful, why the population sifts itself over and over again for the same histories, the same qualities, the same doomed glamour."

O'Connor nods but doesn't write anything. "What conclusion did she come to?" he asks me.

I shake my head, disappointed in him. "Intellectuals do not come to conclusions, Michael," I tell him. "Intellectuals *consider the situation*. That's enough for them."

"And it was enough for you, too?"

"It was paradise," I say. "And yet, almost from the beginning, there were these small signs of trouble ahead."

FLASHBACK 17B

The Malibu kitchen was clean again, once more carefully tended and polished. The television set was gone from the small white table, the fingerprints were gone from the refrigerator, the hanging copper pots gleamed as before, and everything was in its place with a bright shining face.

At the butcher-block island, Jack stood, neatly and absorbedly preparing a peanut butter sandwich on pumpernickel bread. From some other room in the house came a sound rather like a clap or a slap; Jack looked up, attentive, listening, but the sound was not repeated. He returned to his peanut butter and his pumpernickel.

Buddy entered the kitchen, rubbing the side of his face, but when he saw Jack his hand dropped immediately to his side and he forced a kind of careless but lopsided grin, saying, "Hey, how's it goin', Dad?"

Jack smiled at him. "I say Nietzsche was right: Happiness *is* a woman."

Lorraine came into the kitchen, looking grim and flexing the fingers of her right hand. When she saw Jack and

145

Buddy, she dropped her hand to her side, ignored Buddy, and spoke lightly to Jack, saying, "Oh, hello, darling."

"Hello, darling," Jack said.

Buddy was awkward in the presence of these two together. Trying to hide the fact, he scuffed his feet and behaved in an elaborately casual manner. "Well, I'm off," he said, too brightly. "I've been invited to watch the Rams scrimmage. Wanna come along, Dad?"

"Another time, Buddy," Jack said. His eyes and attention were on Lorraine.

"Sure," Buddy said, and did too large a farewell wave, saying, "See you guys."

"So long, Buddy," Jack said, smiling at Lorraine.

Buddy left, his lips twitching, and Lorraine crossed to the butcher-block island, saying with some amusement, "A peanut butter sandwich, darling?"

With an easy laugh, Jack said, "We can't be intellectual *all* the time, darling."

With an easy laugh, Lorraine said, "I only meant, darling, you didn't offer one to *me*."

"Would you like one?" Jack asked her. "Be delighted to make it for you."

"Thank you, darling," Lorraine said, and leaned on the butcher block to watch.

Jack started another sandwich, absorbed and happy in his work. Lorraine watched for a moment, and then said, "Darling?"

Still concentrating on the job at hand, Jack said, "Yes, darling?"

"There's something I don't understand, darling."

"What's that, darling?"

Lorraine hesitated, then went ahead: "Buddy, darling."

With a quizzical laugh, Jack glanced at her, then back at his sandwich-making. "Buddy, darling." he echoed. "What's not to understand about Buddy?"

"His place in your life, darling." Lorraine said, her manner firm.

"Darling," Jack said, "he's my oldest friend in all the world."

"Yes, I know," Lorraine said dryly, "you ate sand to-gether."

Cheered by the memory, Jack said, "Oh, did I tell you about that, darling?"

"Yes, you did, darling." Lorraine took a deep breath, then plunged ahead, saying, "But your relationship with Buddy must have changed since then. You aren't in that sandbox anymore."

"Well, of course not," Jack said, chuckling as though she were making jokes.

"And to a recent arrival on the scene, darling," Lorraine persisted, "it does look awfully as though Buddy is a mere sponge."

"Oh, darling!" Jack said, reproachful.

"A sponge," Lorraine repeated, inexorable. "A wastrel. A parasite. He lives on you, darling, borrows money he never repays, treats your possessions . . . as though he owns them."

"Is it wrong, darling," Jack asked, pleading prettily for understanding, "to be generous to an old friend?"

"It goes beyond generosity," Lorraine insisted. "It's almost as though Buddy had some hold over you, some—"

Quick, urgent, Jack said, "Why do you say that?" And added, as an afterthought, "Darling?"

Casual, not noticing the force of his reaction, she said, "Oh, I don't mean anything as melodramatic as blackmail, darling, as though you'd committed a *murder* or something—" She broke off and looked with some surprise at the sandwich Jack had been making. "Why, darling," she said. "You've stuck the knife right through the bread."

Jack held up the knife, the pumpernickel slice impaled on it. His voice hoarse, he said, "I'll start another sandwich . . . darling."

"But all unknown to all of us, a cloud was hanging over our heads, completely unsuspected. A cloud named Rubelle Kallikak."

FLASHBACK 18

The courtroom, a large traditional place of gleaming dark wood benches and railings, high pale ceiling, large side windows, judge seated on a tall impressive banc flanked by the flags of the United States of America and the state of California, was crowded with onlookers but was almost perfectly still. The six jurors sat in somber intensity, deeply aware of the solemnity and import of their work here. The judge, white-haired, stocky, fatherly, fondled his gavel and gave his full attention to the questioning of the witness.

That witness. The plaintiff, in fact: Rubelle Kallikak. A filthy slattern of seventeen, already spreading in hip and thigh, dressed in cast-off garments a year from their last cleaning, her hair a mare's nest, her nose snot-smeared, her dull eyes a monument to a lifetime of improper diet, she sprawled in the witness chair with a filthy baby shlurping at her sagging breast. Before her was spread the courtroom: in the seats on one side of the aisle her family, dozens of Kallikaks (of whom Rubelle was the beauty), and on the other side the media, eyes and ears wide open.

To her left stood her attorney, a slick-haired sleazeball in a maroon leisure suit and bright blue wide tie. Seated at the defense table were Jack and Lorraine, hand in hand, with their battery of brilliant and expensive lawyers all in pinstripes.

The sleazeball attorney spoke: "And do you, Rubelle Kallikak," he demanded, in a voice which would have been thrilling were it not so nasal, "do you see in this courtroom the man who lavished such promises upon you, ravished you, and left you with child?"

Rubelle waited a moment to be sure the flood of words had spent itself, and then she nodded and smeerped the back of her hand across her nose and nodded again and said, "Uh-huh."

The sleazeball attorney nodded. His worst fears, it seemed, had been realized. "And would, you Rubelle Kallikak, point out to this court and the jury that deceiver?"

Snot glinted from the back of the hand Rubelle raised. Her finger pointed directly at Jack.

The baby started to snivel. Lorraine gave Jack an I'm-with-you pat on the shoulder. Jack smiled at the jury. The jury did not smile back.

am still irritated, years later. "This defective little bitch," I tell O'Connor, "swore she and I spent three days and nights in a riverside cabin up by Stockton. Buddy swore he and I were deer hunting in Colorado all that time. But we didn't have any witnesses—any more than *she* had, the bitch—and Rubelle's lawyer made a big point of Buddy being my closest friend in all the world."

"I vaguely remember that case," O'Connor says, tapping his pen against the notebook. "Several years ago, wasn't it?"

"Fame is fleeting," I point out, this being a sentiment of more than passing interest—fleeting interest?—for me, as you might imagine.

"I don't remember how it came out," O'Connor says.

"*I* do," I say. "Rubelle had three things going for her. Ignorance, poverty, and the general assumption that in all such matters it's the man who's lying. On the other hand, I was encumbered by money, brains, talent, good looks, and the finest legal talent money could buy. I couldn't pretend to be poor or stupid or ugly, and I couldn't very well go out and deliberately hire second-rate attorneys. As you can see, things looked pretty black for me for a while."

"So she won the case?"

"Wait for it, Michael," I say, waving a finger at him. "The fact is, I could see for myself how badly things were going. I could see the way the jury looked at Rubelle, and the way they looked at me. I could read the write-ups in the papers and watch the news reports on television. I saw the slippery slope I was on, and I knew where it ended. So, when it came my turn to testify, I decided on a desperate gamble."

FLASHBACK 18A

The courtroom was just as full as ever, the judge as fatherly as ever, the Kallikaks as numerous and ill-favored as ever, but now it was Jack who sat in the witness box while Rubelle sprawled behind the plaintiff's table, baby vomiting on her heedless breast. One of Jack's highly polished attorneys had just finished leading him through one irrelevant thicket of testimony, was preparing for another similar canter, and had paused beside the defense table, gazing downward, studying his notes with the frown they deserved. Into the little silence thus created, Jack interposed himself, turning his most open and guileless and innocent smile upon the judge, saying, "Your Honor, may I beg the court's indulgence for just a moment?"

The look the judge lowered upon Jack was not fatherly at all, but was truculent, hostile, and terminally unsympathetic. "And just what, Mr. Pine," he wanted to know, "do you and your expensive attorneys have in mind?"

"This is all my idea, Your Honor," Jack said, as his expensive attorney approached the bench, looking worried. "May I proceed?"

"Just a minute, Your Honor," the expensive attorney said, and he turned his unbelieving and disapproving frown upon Jack, saying, "Jack? What are you up to?"

"This won't take long," Jack assured both the judge and the expensive attorney. He turned on the judge his *most* winning smile, saying, "May I, Your Honor, take just a minute? My own idea."

"His own idea, whatever it is," the expensive attorney confirmed, in a voice of doom.

The judge considered. He didn't believe Jack's winning smile for a second, but he *had* to believe the expensive attorney's disapproving frown. "You may proceed," he told Jack, giving the fellow enough rope, and sat back to enjoy the results, whatever they might be.

"Thank you, Your Honor," Jack said, with simple sincerity. Facing the courtroom, raising his voice just a bit, projecting like the stage actor he'd been trained to be, he said, "Lorraine, would you rise, please?"

Lorraine, not knowing what was going on, bewildered that Jack would have come to a plan of action without having first talked it to death with her, uncertainly and with an obvious reluctance got to her feet.

"Thank you," Jack said, and called a bit louder: "Marcia, would you mind, please? Would you rise and come forward and stand next to Lorraine?"

Everyone in the courtroom watched as Marcia Callahan stood from the midst of the spectators—on the media side, not the Kallikak side, which was why she hadn't been noticed before, she could have been just another blond news co-anchor—and walked forward down the aisle. A bailiff opened the gate in the railing, and Marcia stepped through, turning toward Lorraine. Although her career had faltered in the last few years, she was still well enough known to be recognized by just about everybody in court.

Lorraine, watching Marcia approach, did *what's up?* semaphores with her eyebrows, but Marcia merely shrugged and shook her head; she didn't know what was going on, either.

154

Meanwhile, Jack was nodding, reassuring his expensive attorney with little smiles and pats of the hand, and now he spoke up again, calling, "Denise. Angelica. Simone. Would you all come up with Lorraine and Marcia? Just come up and stand beside them."

Three incredibly beautiful women rose from their places in different parts of the courtroom—but all on the media side—and made their way forward. The bailiff's hand shook as he held the gate in the railing open for them, and they passed through, looking about with some curiosity, at one another, at Marcia and Lorraine, and over at Jack, who nodded and smiled and encouraged them with little hand gestures to line up in a row, all five of them.

Once all five were in position, Jack rose and turned to face the jury, which looked at him with hostility and suspicion. Pretending to see nothing but cheery faces, Jack gestured to the five women standing there and said, "Ladies and gentlemen of the jury, that is my present wife, Lorraine, and that is my former wife, the well-known actress, Marcia Callahan."

Expressionless now, the two ladies and four gentlemen of the jury looked at Lorraine and Marcia, and then looked back at Jack.

Who smiled and gestured at the other three women, saying, "Denise and Angelica and Simone are just three of the many attractive and highly intelligent women with whom I have had deliciously satisfying affairs over the last several years on various continents."

Everyone in the room gazed with close concentration on Denise and Angelica and Simone, all three of whom looked startled but game, standing there under all that surveillance. Lorraine and Marcia gave these three new women *very* measuring looks.

Jack's smile now was pitying. He gestured toward the plaintiff's table. "And *there*," he said, "is Miss, uh, Kallikak."

Rubelle removed her infant from one flopping breast with a moist *pop* sound and attached it to the other.

The jury looked at Rubelle. The jury looked at Lorraine and Marcia and Denise and Angelica and Simone.

Jack spread his hands. "Ladies and gentlemen of the jury," he said, ". . . I ask you."

"But, I don't know," I tell O'Connor, shaking my head at the memory, "sometimes you can't win for losing."

FLASHBACK 17C

Into the booklined airy living room of the Malibu house came Jack and Lorraine, arguing, she coldly furious, he bewildered but beginning to get sore. "Darling," he said, as they entered the room, "we *won.*"

"But despicably, darling," Lorraine said through clenched teeth. "I've never seen such utter and total male-chauvinist piggery in my entire life."

"Would you rather we had *lost*?" Jack demanded. "Would you have liked that no-doubt brain-damaged infant to have been a part of our *lives* from now on? Would you have liked it to *live* with us?"

"We have to live with ourselves, darling," Lorraine said, cold and furious, her face dead-white except for two high splotches of color.

Buddy entered the room from deeper in the house before Jack could think of the proper response. Grinning from ear to ear, Buddy spread his arms wide and marched across the room toward Jack as to a conquering hero. "Congratulations, Dad!" he cried. "It was on the radio."

"Thanks, Buddy," Jack said, beginning to smile, turning with relief to this evidence of approval.

Buddy wrapped his arms around Jack and gave him a bear hug, grinning over Jack's shoulder at Lorraine, saying, "What do you think of our boy, Lorraine?"

Lorraine didn't answer. Buddy's grin became knowing, while Jack's shoulder blades tightened as he became aware of the lengthening silence. At last, he disengaged himself from Buddy and turned to see Lorraine studying them both, her expression enigmatic, thoughtful, calculating. "Darling?" Jack said, unable to keep the anxiety out of his voice. "What are you thinking, darling?"

"I'm thinking, *darling*," Lorraine said slowly but emphatically, "that you two probably do deserve each other, but I don't deserve either of you."

Thunderstruck, Jack cried, "Darling! You aren't leaving me!"

"Oh, but I am, darling," Lorraine said, with the calm confidence of someone whose mind is made up at last. "But before I go, there's just one thing—"

Jack ducked and leaped over the nearest sofa. He stood behind it, alert, ready for anything. Lorraine ignored this odd behavior, ignored everything except her own exit line: "Just one thing I want to tell you," she said. "Buddy Pal, your oldest friend in all the world, several times in the course of our marriage tried to rape me. Fortunately, I minored in judo."

Having delivered her exit line, she turned about, square-shouldered, and made her exit. Jack, staring at her back, coming out from behind the sofa, shrillness in his voice, cried, "You're just trying to make trouble!"

Lorraine kept going. A door closed, not forcefully. Jack turned his wide-eyed stare on Buddy, who shrugged and grinned, completely at his ease. "That bag of bones?" Buddy said. "Not my type, Dad, you know me."

Jack continued to stare at him, not responding, not changing in any way. Buddy crossed to him, the same crooked confident grin on his face, and gave Jack a light but meaningful tap on the arm, saying, "You *do* know me, Dad, remember? From the very *first* girl. Remember?"

Jack was slow to answer, his breathing strained, muscles jumping in his cheeks, but at last he sagged, and his face lost its tension, and he said, "I remember, Buddy."

Buddy nodded, secure, and tapped Jack's arm again. Then he turned away, crossing toward the liquor cabinet, saying, "You won a big case today, Dad. Want a little drink to celebrate?"

"Yes," Jack said. He hadn't yet moved.

Buddy opened the liquor cabinet and held up a bottle of Jack Daniel's. "On the rocks, or straight up?"

At last Jack moved. He crossed the room, saying, "Don't wrap it, I'll drink it here." Taking the bottle from Buddy's hand, he removed the top, threw it away behind himself, put the bottle to his mouth, leaned his head back, and chugalugged.

"That was when I started hitting the bottle pretty heavy."

O'Connor looks at me, as though not sure whether to believe what I'm saying. "You mean," he asks, "you weren't a drinker before your second marriage broke up?"

"I was a social drinker," I tell him, and shrug. "Like anybody else." (Hey, I just shrugged there and didn't fall over! I'm getting better, health is returning, I can feel it. Once again, I survive the Temple of Doom.) "But after Lorraine left," I continue, "I wasn't a social drinker, I was a *drinker*. And it was beginning to affect my work."

FLASHBACK 19

The antiques-store set was wide but shallow with an old glass-paned door leading to a minimal sidewalk set at the right end, and smaller, darker wooden door leading out of the left end to nowhere but the rest of the soundstage. The effect in the film would be of a deep narrow dark shop, crammed with all sorts of curios.

Facing this set broadside were the usual crew and equipment. The director, a florid stocky bald man in a bush jacket, sat on a tall canvas-backed stool beside the camera. "Quiet," he said, quietly.

"Quiet!" called an AD.

"Quiet!" called a further-off AD.

"Rolling," murmured the director.

"Rolling!" called the first AD.

"Rolling!" screamed the further-off AD.

Nothing happened.

The director looked sardonic and long-suffering. Shifting position on his stool, he raised his voice a bit and called, "We're rolling, Jack. That's your cue."

Still nothing happened.

The director looked as sardonic, but even more long-suffering. Speaking generally, to ADs, grips, best boys, gaffers, script girls, whoever might know anything of use, he said, "Jack? Is he back there?"

No one spoke. A general awful embarrassment rose from the assembled company like shimmering heat waves. The director, masterfully combining deference with irritation in his voice, called, "Jack? We are rolling now, Jack."

The front door of the antiques shop burst open, slamming back against the set wall. Jack reeled in, off balance, the door having weighed less than it looked so that he'd given it a little too much push when he'd opened it, and then he'd tried to overcompensate in the other direction, and now all he was trying to do was stay on his feet.

His waving arms sent a candelabra flying toward the camera, bouncing on the floor at the director's feet. Next, a stuffed owl was knocked the other way off a crowded shelf, taking a kerosene lantern along with a crash and a clatter.

The sudden noise startled Jack just as he was getting his equilibrium back, and he staggered sideways into a row of porcelain beer steins, sending them into and through a display of old doll furniture. Lunging away from all that, Jack became entangled with an old wooden rocking chair, fought manfully to free himself from the thing, and only succeeded by reducing the rocking chair to kindling, some of which swept nearby shelves clean of apothecary bottles, tea sets, samovars, and stereopticons.

Each move Jack made caused a separate and distinct crash, smash, thunk, tinkle, thud, bang, crumple, snap, jingle, gong, crack, and/or pit-a-pat, and every noise made Jack try again to correct his course by making another move. Thus, by an irregular series of tattoos, detonations, and dying falls, he crossed the set from right to left. Never quite toppling over, never quite getting his balance, never quite managing to just stand still, Jack swept like the angel of death across the antiques shop set, leaving hurricane news footage in his wake.

At the far end of the set, he brought up against the interior door, which was not in fact a working door at all, so that he didn't pass through it but merely brought up hard against it, with force enough to make the whole set tremble. Recoiling from this encounter, he reeled back through his previous carnage to the middle of the set, where at last he managed to come to something like a stop; though he trembled all over, like a race horse after the meet.

And he wasn't quite finished yet. Turning to say something to the director, raising one expressive hand, index finger upthrust, he lost his balance yet again. This time, he tottered backward, feet fumbling and stumbling with the shards and shreds of his previous passage, until he reached the wall of the set. Here he flung his arms out to the sides as though crucified and leaned back against the wall, which gave way, the whole canvas rear wall of the set slowly falling over, Jack riding it down backward, arms outspread, an expression of harried but mild surprise on his face as he and the wall went completely over and landed with a mighty *whoosh* and great puffs of dust.

No one said a word. A final *clink* was heard from somewhere. The dust slowly settled. And then the director spoke. "Cut," he said.

"But I didn't care, not then. As long as I was drunk, I just thought life was one big party."

FLASHBACK 20

Another transformation had come to the living room of the house in Malibu. The books and bookcases were gone, as though they had never been. The furniture, pushed back against the walls, was scruffier, showing signs of hard wear. Five television sets in various parts of the room were all switched on, but the sounds they might have been making were impossible to hear because the room was *jammed* with partygoers: a young and hedonistic crowd, laughing and shouting, scoffing down the bottomless supply of liquor and the endlessly refilled side table of finger foods. Jack reeled among his guests, a glazed look in his eyes and a glazed smile on his face. He held a quart bottle of Jack Daniel's Black Label by the neck and paused from time to time to knock back a slug.

Buddy moved toward Jack through the partygoers. He was sober, neatly dressed in pale sports jacket and open-necked shirt, and in his eyes was a faint expression of disapproval of the scene swirling around him. That expression disappeared when he reached the sozzled Jack, to be replaced by his usual look of aggressive and self-confident comradeship. Never had the familial similarity between these two been less noticeable; Buddy was trim and neat, clearly in good physical shape, while Jack was getting jowly, his body sagging within his rumpled clothing. The parallels between them had become obscured by their very different ways of caring for themselves.

"*Hey*, Buddy!" Jack called, seeing his oldest friend, turning to stagger toward him. "*Hey*, my Buddy!"

"Listen, Dad," Buddy said, low and confidential, "could I have the car?"

"*Sure*, Buddy." Jack frisked himself with uncertain gestures, switching the bottle from hand to hand, until he found a set of car keys, which he handed over.

Buddy nodded, pocketing the keys, but said, "No, Dad, I meant could I have the *car*."

"Whuzza?"

Buddy brought out of his inside jacket pocket automotive sale documents and a pen. Leading Jack to a nearby table, spreading the papers on it, handing Jack the pen, he said, "Just sign here, Dad. You see, I got a little something to take care of south of the border."

"Oh, sure, Buddy," Jack said. An amiable drunk, he put the bottle down, scrawled his name with a flourish, dropped the pen, picked the bottle up, and drank.

Buddy retrieved documents and pen. "Thanks, Dad," he said, patted Jack on the shoulder, and left.

A girl who'd been sitting on the sofa beside the table grinned up at Jack and said, "Hey, baby. You got a car for me?"

"That's my oldest friend in all the world," Jack told her.

"Yeah?" the girl said. "He doesn't look that old."

Jack thought about that, nodding, smiling in a distracted way, and then he got it, and it *broke him up*. His eyes came to life! His smile beamed like the sun! His arms shot up! He slopped Tennessee sour mash whiskey all over the place! He yelled, "Oh, wow! Holy—oh, gee!"

"It wasn't *that* good," the girl said, beginning to get worried.

"Wasn't—Comere! Comere!"

Jack dragged the girl up off the sofa and threw his arm around her shoulders. While she held her head drawn as far as possible away from him, looking sideways at his manic profile with only semicomic revulsion and alarm, he dragged her toward the hot center of the party, crying, "Hey, come here! Hey, listen to this! *Wit?* Holy shit!"

"**B**ut it all came to a head the night I won my Academy Award."

FLASHBACK 21

"**A**nd now, to present the award for Best Actor, *Dori Lunsford!*"

The band played. The audience applauded. The billions watching on television all around the world watched Dori Lunsford approach the lectern. A big-boned, good-looking blonde, Dori Lunsford was the sex symbol of the moment, a big girl whose stock in trade was giggly little-girl movements, as though she didn't know she was voluptuous. Tonight she wore an extremely low-cut white gown, the hot television lights gleaming on the upper hemispheres of her breasts.

At the lectern, she bowed slightly, presenting those breasts to the world, or at least the half of the world watching her on television. The plain forgettable man from Price Waterhouse—rather like Michael O'Connor he was, in fact—came out and handed Dori Lunsford the envelope and went away again, immediately forgotten.

"Oh, I'm so excited!" Dori told the billions, and jiggled a little. (She was having her period, which always made her breasts swell.) Tearing open the envelope with a pleasing clumsiness, she said, "And the winner isssss . . ." She pulled the card most of the way from the envelope, and *squealed*. "EEEEEEEEEEEE!!! *Jack Pine!*"

In the audience, as it burst into applause, competing with the band's breaking into the theme music of the film for which Jack was getting his award, Buddy poked at Jack, who was sound asleep in the aisle seat beside him. Knowing he was on television, Buddy did his poking with a good-natured grin on his lips, as though congratulating his pal rather than waking him, but his knuckles were hard and sharp, digging into Jack's ribs, yanking him unpleasurably up from alcoholic stupor.

Jack roused himself, hearing the confused noises, seeing the lights, feeling Buddy's sharp fists prod him up out of the seat and into the aisle. "Go on, Dad!" Buddy yelled, through the music and applause. "Go get it!"

Befuddled but moving, Jack made his way down the aisle. Like a rat in a maze, he was constricted to this route by the applauding hands and beaming faces on both sides. Sensing the urgency all around him, he broke into a shambling trot, found himself abruptly in front of steps, and ran up them only because the alternative would have been to sprawl across them in a painful heap.

At the top of the stairs, Jack hesitated for just a second, unsure what he was supposed to do next, having not the slightest idea what was going on. Several tuxedoed and gowned people behind a curtain, within his line of sight but out of camera range, stopped applauding to wave at him frantically to hang a left and get *going*. He hung a left. He got going.

And here was Dori Lunsford. And here was some sort of elbow-height piece of furniture to lean on. Feeling an intense need to lean on something, Jack approached that piece of furniture, but before he could get his body on it Dori Lunsford smiled like the sun in Bangkok and handed him something. Jack grasped at it, whatever it was, and Dori kissed his cheek, pressing her great globes against his arm and chest.

Jack weaved slightly, not leaning against anything. He

looked at the shiny thing in his hands and recognized it, but didn't quite yet dope out its meaning or implications. With a piteous look at Dori, begging for enlightenment, he said, "This is for me?"

The microphone on the lectern picked up the question, of course. The audience, which had quieted enough to hear what Jack might say, naturally thought it was meant to be a joke, and responded with good-natured laughter and more applause. Jack looked out toward the great hall, saw it full of people, and began to catch on. He looked back at Dori. He had it together now, and his trouper's spirit took over.

The famous Jack Pine smile flashed. The famous Jack Pine voice spoke: "Well, thank you, Dori."

At which point, Dori was supposed to leave, backing smiling away from the lectern to give the recipient of the award his opportunity to thank everybody on God's green earth for having made this moment possible. Preparatory to this rearward departure, Dori did smile her farewell smile, but then something went wrong. Jack reached out his right hand—the left hand still clutching Oscar about the head, as though he were a bottle of Jack Daniel's—dipped the hand into the open top of Dori's dress, and grasped her right, or downstage, breast.

Dori gasped. The whole audience gasped, but Dori gasped on television. Dori started to pull away, to make her scheduled departure anyway, but then she realized—as her expression told the half of the world's population watching—that she'd better not.

With his left hand clutching Oscar and his right hand clutching Dori's breast, Jack turned toward an audience suddenly grown deathly still. "And thank all of you," he said. "I mean it, honest to God I do."

Dori stood frozen, a terrified smile on her face. She had no choice but to remain there throughout Jack's acceptance speech, and in her panic she had clearly come to the conclusion that the best thing to do was look as happy and bubbly as possible, just as though nothing had gone terribly wrong, just as though her breast was not now in the tight and unrelenting grip of a madman.

Jack went on, addressing the audience, saying, "I really thank you all for this, uh, Tony, Emmy, what the hell is it?" He held up the statuette, studied it closely. "Oscar," he decided. Lowering the statuette again, but still holding on to Dori, he looked out at the oil painting of an audience and said, "I thank you. And I want to thank everybody who made this moment possible. I want to thank every ass I ever had to kiss. I want to thank every prick who ever turned me down for a rotten picture so I was forced to do the good ones. I want to thank Marty Friedman, my director, that traffic cop, for staying the hell away from me and letting me get the job done. And I want to thank my co-star, Sandra Shaw, for doing such a tight-ass, piss-poor, lamebrain job of it that I *had* to look good in comparison. You notice *she* didn't get a nomination. But mostly, I want to thank all those little people out there, all those little people out there, those little people, all those goddamn little people. There's more of them around all the time, you know? I think they live in the plumbing."

Finished, befuddled again, his mind full of lurking, crawling, slithering little people, Jack turned and walked off stage, leaving a stunned silence behind, but taking Dori Lunsford along by the breast.

"**S**ix weeks later, I married that bitch."

Michael O'Connor is at last surprised by something. "Dori Lunsford?" he says. "I didn't know you were ever married to Dori Lunsford."

A flaw in his impeccable research, eh? I smile at him in triumph—we keep our secrets, yes we do, when we want, large and small—and I say, "It didn't last."

"I guess it didn't."

I lean forward slightly, feeling extremely healthy, a sound body in a sound mind—no, that's the other way around, isn't it? Doesn't matter—and I rest my elbows on my spread knees, and I gaze into the middle distance of time. "How different that was," I say, "from my first wedding, even though they both took place in the same church."

"Same church?" O'Connor echoes. "Isn't that unusual?"

"Very photogenic church," I explain. "Great for the press. You fellas. Well, *you* know that. And this time, of course, we didn't have to hire a crowd. We both had our

174

fans, our agents, household staffs, attorneys, accountants, stand-ins, hangers-on, the whole crowd. The media was out in force, a lot more so than when Marcia and I tied the knot. We all had to work our asses off to suppress *those* pictures, let me tell you."

"Pictures?" O'Connor looks bewildered, poor fella; I'm surprised he doesn't already know this part, being in the journalism racket and all. He says, "Suppress pictures? What pictures?"

"Of the wedding," I tell him.

Which doesn't seem to help him much. Shaking his head as though there's a bee in his ear, he says, "Suppress pictures of the wedding. Your old wedding with Marcia, you mean? So people wouldn't know it was the same church?"

"Oh, who cares about that?" I ask him. "One of the very few good qualities of the press is that it has no memory. No, it was the pictures of the wedding with *Dori* we had to suppress. And a hell of a job it was, too."

"I don't understand," he confesses. "If the whole thing was meant to be a publicity stunt, why suppress the pictures?"

"Because things went a little bit wrong," I explain.

"What things?"

"Well, we were *both* of us drinking pretty heavy then," I tell him. "It was the only way we could put up with each other, or anything else, or get through the day. So, we handled the ceremony okay, but on the way back down the aisle—or is it back *up* the aisle?—anyway, on our way back from the altar, Dori's drunk said something that irritated my drunk just a little."

FLASHBACK 22

The lovely white chapel in Santa Monica had been freshly painted for the occasion, and parts of the gleaming green grass had been resodded. Hundreds and hundreds of wedding guests and media people milled about in front of the chapel, held back from the gray cement walk leading from front steps to street by police sawhorses and stern-looking, blue uniformed, white helmeted policemen. A red carpet had been unrolled from the church door down the steps and across the gray cement walk and the sidewalk to the waiting limo. Organ music and the sound of an expensive imported choir rang out from within as the ushers opened the twin front doors.

Jack and Dori came out, he in tux, she in a different white gown from the one she'd worn to the Academy Awards, this one showing a bit less cleavage. Jack and Dori were yelling and screaming at each other, both red-faced, both waving their arms around. Jack shoved Dori when they reached the top step, but instead of falling, Dori swung around and smashed him across the head with her bouquet. He then took a swing at her, but she ducked and kicked him in the shin.

Ushers and friends, paralyzed with shock in the first few seconds, at last hurried forward to break up the newly-weds, both of whom now swung and missed, Jack's overhand right taking out a flower girl, while Dori's left uppercut sent an usher flying off the steps and into the crowd below. Jack finally connected with a straight left to Dori's forehead, driving her back into an off-balance wedding guest, who in his turn fell backward into two photographers, who shoved him unceremoniously out of the way. The wedding guest, not taking kindly to this opening of a second front at his rear, turned around and popped a photographer. So then the second photographer popped the wedding guest. So then another wedding guest popped the second photographer.

Jack and Dori meanwhile, weaving and staggering in the church doorway, had entered upon a hair-and-clothes-ripping contest, their elbows and knees doing much damage among those well-wishers who tried to intervene. And the more people were knocked off the steps into the people below, the more the fight spread.

In no time at all, it had become a general brawl, its turmoil reverberating out from the epicenter of the happy couple. Policemen and police sawhorses alike were trampled into the fresh sod as the fight spilled over onto the lawn, engulfing more and more of the wedding guests and then the media people, and then the fans, extending even into the two TV remote vans parked just down the block. The limo driver, seeing which way the wind was blowing and not expecting his fares to make it to curbside today anyway, decided to get his vehicle out of the danger zone, but in moving it he made both the car and himself moving targets, obvious and irritating to the mob at large. Although he locked himself in, and the crowd never did get at him, the limo itself was never the same again and shortly thereafter was sold for cash to a Columbian who wanted the comforts of air-conditioning and television while overseeing the work of his farm in the uplands.

As the brawl spread to the street, cars and trucks, blocked in their passage, disgorged their drivers and passengers to enter into the fray. A school bus full of bored teenagers on their way back to school from a field trip to the La Brea tarpits added its own dollop of youthful enthusiasm to the developing stew.

Jack and Dori, both off their feet now, clutched in each other's violent embrace, kicked and bit and scratched and punched and rolled around on the red carpet among the feet of the nearer brawlers. Being down there, intent on their pummeling, each with an earlobe of the other clenched in their teeth, they were among the last to hear the wail of the approaching sirens.

"**W**e were going to honeymoon in Brazil," I tell O'Connor, "but the marriage didn't last that long, so I went with Buddy instead."

So many things startle and perplex this fellow. He goggles at me. "You had the honeymoon anyway?" he demands. "With *Buddy*?"

"Well," I explain, "it was never going to be *just* a honeymoon, anyway. It was always going to be a deductible expense."

He doesn't get that part either. "A trip to Brazil? A honeymoon in Brazil? With or without the bride? A deductible expense?"

He is beginning to astonish me as much as I'm astonishing him. For a media maven, he sure as hell doesn't know much. I say, "Don't you know what Brazil's famous for?"

"Coffee," he says.

"No."

"Inflation."

"No."

"Brazil nuts?"

"Faces," I tell him.

His face is one of which they would never approve. He gapes at me with it. "Faces?"

"They've got a clinic down there," I tell him. "It's the most complete plastic-surgery operation in the world."

"In Brazil?"

"Absolutely. Plastic surgery to the stars; that's where it's done. Any operation you can think of and some you probably can't. Everybody goes there."

"I didn't know that," he says.

Feeling kindly toward him, I explain as gently as I can: "That's because you're nobody."

Not quite gentle enough, perhaps. Looking and sounding snippy, he says, "I'd always thought there were any number of plastic surgeons right here in Los Angeles."

"Oh, sure," I say. "Anybody can get hacked away at by those Bev Hills butchers, but if you want to be taken seriously in the industry, your face and body better say MADE IN BRAZIL."

"I never guessed," he says.

"I tell you, Michael," I say, "I've had a standing reservation forever. I go down once a year, talk it over with the doctors, see what we want to snip and tuck."

"You've had plastic surgery?" He's peering at me, looking quite surprised at the idea.

"Are you kidding?" I ask him. "At my age, with the life I've led, there's only two ways I could look the way I do: either a painting in the attic, or a plastic surgeon in Brazil. I go Brazil."

"Gosh," he says.

"You bet. Every spring, I arrange it so my time's free, I fly on down to Rio and take in the carnival, and then go on to the clinic for the overhaul. Then back I come, feeling great, looking great, ready for another year of self-abuse."

"So that's where you planned to go with Dori Lunsford for your honeymoon."

"Right. The doctors could have worked on the both of us

at the same time. Dori was getting a little flabby around the edges; she needed tightening up."

"But when the marriage ended, you went with Buddy instead."

"The last few years, Buddy's been coming down with me every time." I chuckle, thinking of how serious Buddy can be when he puts his mind to it. "He really pays attention down there." I say. "Takes notes, talks with the doctors, observes the operations. Not me; I don't want to see what faces look like when they're open."

"But Buddy does."

"I kid him sometimes," I say. "When he's around and not mad at me, you know?"

"Buddy gets mad at you?"

"Oh, nothing serious," I say. "He worries about me, that's all. *You* know what I mean." But this conversation is making me edgy. Some sort of dark cloud is coming up from between the pieces of patio slate, swirling up, enveloping me. But it's not a bad cloud, not an evil cloud, no; it's a friendly cloud. It is here to help me, protect me, save me.

"Well, what do you kid Buddy about?" O'Connor is asking me, as the cloud rises between us. "During those times when he isn't mad at you, what do you kid him about?"

"That he's gonna know as much about the plastic surgery as the doctors pretty soon," I say, "and I won't have to go down there every spring; I can stay here and Buddy can do the nips and the tucks."

"He's that interested, is he?"

The cloud is obscuring everything. I try to remember what we're talking about. Brazil. "I'm about due," I say, reaching up and patting the back of my hand against the underpart of my chin, feeling the looseness there. "I may have to start going twice a year," I say. "Well, it's been nice talking to you," I say, and I enter the cloud.

LUDE

At first, O'Connor has no idea what's happened. Pine was talking along, being coherent, making as much sense as he's ever made today, and then all at once he said, "It's been nice talking to you," and he smiled and waved by-by, and now he's just sitting there, unmoving. His eyes are glazed, his mouth holds a loose vague smile, and his hands rest easily in his lap. He is sitting up and his eyes are open, but he isn't home.

"Mr. Pine?" O'Connor says, and repeats it louder: "Mr. Pine? Shit, again?" Shaking his head, he yells, "Hoskins!"

And that worthy appears at once, stepping rapidly from the house, hurrying this way, carrying in his right hand the familiar silver tray bearing a single tall glass of water, and in his left hand an old black doctor's bag. Arriving, "You bellowed, sir?" he asks.

O'Connor indicates the frozen actor. "You see."

Hoskins studies this latest manifestation. "Ah, yes," he says. "I thought we might go next to Middle Earth. Particularly if we were feeling threatened or upset."

"Maybe so," O'Connor says. "I thought maybe we were finally getting somewhere. Can you bring him out of it?"

182

With cheery indomitability, Hoskins says, "Trust to luck, eh?"

O'Connor sits back, notebook resting in his lap, and watches Hoskins go to one knee, put the tray bearing the glass of water to one side on the patio slate, and open the doctor's bag. For some little time he studies its contents, then frowns at O'Connor, saying, "How much longer will you need him?"

"Hard to say, exactly," O'Connor answers, tapping his pen against the notebook.

"Less than an hour?"

"Oh, sure," O'Connor says. "No problem."

"Good," Hoskins says. "All in all, one prefers not to use the suppositories."

As Hoskins begins taking bottles and boxes from the bag, studying them, fiddling with them, O'Connor says, "Hoskins, do you have to keep readjusting him all the time like this?"

"Oh, no, sir," Hoskins assures him. "Usually we let him set his own pace, you know. It's only if he's actually filming, or such. But today, of course, is rather different."

"I see." O'Connor nods, then says, "Hoskins, do you mind my asking? What do you *think* of Jack Pine?"

"Think of him, sir?" Hoskins ponders that question, then says, "One doesn't normally *think* about one's employer. It's not quite seemly. Still, I would say he's rather easier than most to get along with."

"Particularly when he's like this," O'Connor suggests.

"Too true," Hoskins agrees. "Nevertheless, he is rather a sweet person at heart." Frowning at the sweet person, Hoskins says, "Our next adjustment is a two-stager. Do you mind my being here in the interval?"

"You mean, while I'm questioning him?"

"Well, yes, sir, or whatever you do."

"Is that necessary?" O'Connor asks. He seems jealous of his privileged privacy with the actor.

"You could perhaps do the second part yourself, sir, if you wouldn't object," Hoskins suggests.

"No objection," O'Connor says promptly. "What do I do?"

"You have a watch?"

"Sure," O'Connor says, extending his left wrist, showing the Timex strapped there.

"Good."

Hoskins places the tray bearing the glass of water next to O'Connor's chair. He transfers three red capsules from a bottle out of the doctor's bag to his palm and then to the tray, next to the water. "When I give you the sign," he says, "look at your watch, and in exactly three minutes from that time, give him these three capsules. Make sure he takes them all and washes them down with all the water. We don't want him going nova on us."

"No, you're right," O'Connor says. Feeling something like awe, he looks at his watch and at the three capsules lying on the silver tray.

From the doctor's bag, Hoskins takes a plastic tube with a ball at the end of it. There seems to be something inside the tube, which Hoskins inserts into Pine's left nostril. Then he slowly squeezes the ball, counting aloud: "One. Two. Three. Four. *Five*." Removing the tube from his employer's nose, he turns and says to O'Connor, "Counting from *now*."

O'Connor looks closely at his watch. He's very aware of his responsibility.

Hoskins puts the tube away, puts the other boxes and bottles away, and closes the doctor's bag. Then he gets to his feet, dusts off the knees of his trousers, picks up the doctor's bag, and says to O'Connor, "Remember, sir. Three minutes."

"I remember," O'Connor says.

Pine suddenly speaks, without altering his posture or expression or changing in any other way. In a deep sepulchral voice he says, "Frankly, Scarlett, I don't give a flying fuck."

"Ah, yes," Hoskins says, nodding in satisfaction. "The *Gone with the Wind* remake. We just recently completed that."

184

"I know," O'Connor says. "He told me."

"More of it may surface," Hoskins says, "but it should taper off quite soon."

In that same deep sepulchral voice, still without shifting position or changing facial expression, the actor intones, "You want something from me, and you want it badly enough to show a lot of tit in those velvets."

"Well," Hoskins says, "until the next crisis." And he leaves, heading back to the house again, carrying the doctor's bag with him.

O'Connor, mindful of the three-minute deadline, looks at his watch.

"What time is it?"

Startled, O'Connor looks past his watch at the actor, and finds the man looking back at him, calm and relaxed and apparently in perfectly ordinary shape. O'Connor says, "Mr. Pine? Are you all right?"

"Of course I'm all right," Pine answers, his manner now surly, even snappish. "Who the hell are you?" he demands. "You better scram before I call Security."

"I'm Michael O'Connor. We've been talking here."

Pine's face goes blank. In that deep sepulchral voice again, he says, "Rhett. Rhett Butler. And I don't take shit from any man."

Exasperated, trying to find some way to get Pine back on track, O'Connor says, "Did Dori Lunsford get the beach house? After the divorce?"

The actor frowns at him, uncomprehending, and slowly that expressive face changes, lightens up, becomes cheerful and welcoming again. "The interviewer!" Pine says, delighted to see him. "Where you been, Michael?"

O'Connor, becoming wise in the ways of Jack Pine's mind, says, "Took a walk around, looked at the property."

"Nice here, isn't it?" Pine smiles around at his land, and O'Connor notices how he manages never to look directly at the swimming pool. Still smiling, the actor says, "No, it was Lorraine who got the beach house, finally, after a long fight. Dori would have gotten *this* place, only we didn't actually have to get divorced."

185

"You didn't?"

"No." The actor smiles broadly in remembered pleasure. "It was a real pleasant surprise. I got an annulment, not a divorce. Turns out, prenuptial consummations don't count."

"So this has been your home ever since."

Pine looks around, looks left, looks right, smiles in comfortable ownership, never looks directly at the pool. "Yeah," he says dreamily. "There's no place like home."

DREAM SEQUENCE

A heavenly chorus sings; hallelujah. Jack floats down the wide staircase, a dust mote among the dust motes, his fingertips gliding down the polished oak balustrade, his feet never touching the stairs. Shafts of sunlight bend around him, creating a personal monogrammed rainbow just for Jack Pine. Imagine!

Partway down the stairs, Jack meets sullen, grumpy old Buddy coming up, in loafers and chinos and a beautiful beige cashmere sweater that just eats up all the sun. "*Hi*, Buddy," Jack sings, pirouetting on the stairs, the chorus turning his words into madrigals, the dust motes writing the music on the staffs of sunshafts. "Just get in, Buddy Buddy?"

"Looks that way," grumbles Buddy, not in tune with the music or the day at all, and he stumps on up the stairs, barely even glancing in Jack's direction.

Why can't Buddy be happy? *Jack* is happy. Jack floats down a step or two, then stops to consider a sudden kind of revelation. Wafting about, gazing upward at Buddy's bent receding back, Jack says, "Buddy? Isn't that my sweater?"

"It was," Buddy says, without pausing or looking back. As Jack watches, with tiny tendrils of distress creeping about his heart, Buddy pounds on up to the top of the stairs and disappears down the wide white hall.

"Sir?"

It is Hoskins's voice, taking a solo above the chorus. Jack floats around to face down-flight, and there stands Hoskins, all in black, at the bottom step, his hand upon the newel post.

"Ah, Hoskins," Jack breathes, grateful for the distraction that made him forget . . .

. . . something.

"Dr. Ovoid's here, sir," Hoskins announces.

Elation lifts Jack even farther into the air, inches and inches above the mundane wooden steps. "Goody!" he cries.

Hoskins lifts a surprisingly expressive hand from the newel post and gestures gracefully with it, as he says, "I put him in the east parlor."

"Oh, yes! Oh, yes! The east parlor!" And Jack sails through the air, over Hoskins's surprised and laughing head, sweeping away toward the east parlor.

Within the east parlor, waiting, looms Dr. Ovoid, large and round and sleek and buttery and well-satisfied, with a dead-white face and tiny hands and feet. The east parlor itself is a lovely room, full of flowers and morning sun and white wicker furniture; but at the moment Dr. Ovoid stands by a prettily curtained window, smiling as he gazes out upon the rose garden in rich and luxuriant flower. And behind him, on a long table, rests a rolled-up black silk bag a bit larger and much softer than a quart whiskey bottle.

The hall door swings open of its own accord, and in a moment Jack swirls in, surrounded by fairy garlands and cherubs trilling hosannahs. "Good *morrrr*-ning, doctor," sings Jack, and in great good spirits he flies around the ceiling.

Dr. Ovoid turns and beams upon his patient, happy to see this happiness, happy to be appreciated, happy to be *wanted*. "Good morning, Jack," he says, and rubs his tiny hands together, and paces to the long table.

While Jack eagerly watches, dancing in place, the doctor's tiny fingers untie the silk ribbon holding the silk bag closed. Then he unrolls the bag down the length of the table, showing the coral-colored silk lining within. The silk bag is like a half-size sleeping bag, one foot wide and three feet long, and its interior is lined with compartments displaying bottles of pills, bottles of powders, boxes of capsules and ampules, packages of inhalers and suppositories, all sorts of wonderful things for good little boys and girls. "Living better chemically," Jack says, rubbing his hands together, smiling down at the assortment.

Dr. Ovoid steps back and spreads his hands like a showman, displaying his wares. "Well, Jack," he says. "And how do you want to feel today?"

LUDE CONTINUED

O'Connor watches Jack Pine's dreamy eyes, dreamy smile. Will the man ever get down to it, get to the point? But the closer he comes to present time, of course, the harder it becomes to keep him moving. "There's no place like home," O'Connor says, repeating the actor's last words in an effort to get him in motion again.

"Ohhhh, yes." Those dreamy eyes find O'Connor's eyes and gaze into them. "I'm safe here," says that dreamy voice.

"The world's left outside."

"Yeeessss." The eyes are filling with color, becoming less dreamy. "It's very nice here, very restful," and the voice gets stronger, the words faster, "after a hard day at the studio." The voice is going up in pitch, the eyes are pinholes in a decaying face, the words are coming faster and faster: "I can warm my flank, create a cause by the crater of the Susanna sometimewhenthesoonsunsome-soonsunsooooooOOOOOO—!!"

"Oh, my God!" O'Connor cries, lost in the actor's keening. "The pills!"

"YYYYYYYYYYYYYYYYYYYYYYYYYYYYYYYYYYYYYYYY!!!!!"

Fumbling in haste, O'Connor blunders out of his canvas chair and onto his knees beside the dead-faced, pin-eyed screaming actor. His nervous fingers chase the three red capsules around the silver tray like an overeager puppy snuffling after ants on the sidewalk. He manages to capture all three, fold them into his palm.

"YYYYYYYYYY—"

O'Connor clutches the back of Pine's neck with one hand, shoves the capsules with his other hand down into that black and red straining screaming maw, reaches for the waterglass.

"Y! Y! Y! Y! Y!"

O'Connor pours water into that mouth; some bubbles out again, over the actor's chin and down onto his pale blue terry-cloth robe, but some stays, oozing past the screams and down the gullet.

"Y-ng! *Y*-ng! *Y*-ng! Y-ng! ngngngngngngngngng-ngng . . ."

O'Connor, still kneeling, still holding the waterglass— now half empty—sits back on his heels and watches. The noises from the actor's mouth lessen, become arrhythmic, more like burps or hiccups or dry leaves. O'Connor, his brow furrowed with guilt and fellow-feeling, says, "Mr. Pine? Jack?"

The actor grows silent. Then, all at once, he shudders all over his body, as though reacting to some strong explosion deep within. After an instant of rigidity, he begins to tremble, as though freezing cold, and a look of terror crosses his face. Folding his shoulders in defensively toward his ears, he brings his knees up to his chin and wraps his arms around his legs. The look of terror increases, becomes a rigid stare into the deepest pit, and in a small, cracking, weak, tremulous voice the actor says, "That—That—That—That can—That can . . . *hurt*."

"I'm sorry," O'Connor tells him, with utter sincerity, and risks touching the actor on the arm. "I'm really sorry. I forgot the time."

Pine still stares at nothing, his head twitching from time

191

to time. He seems to be talking mostly to himself. "That can—" he says, and trembles, and says, "hurt. Oh, boy. That can hurt. Oh. *Hurt.*"

"Sorry. Really." O'Connor gets up off his knees and resumes his old position in the chair, reclaiming his pen and notebook from where he'd dropped them on the slate in that moment of panic. His expression still worried, he watches the actor's slow recovery.

Pine, crouched over his upraised knees, rubs his arms obsessively. His breathing, which had been quick and strained, grows more level, more even. He turns his head slowly, looks at O'Connor as though he can actually see him, then looks away again, at whatever it is he sees at the farthest range of infinity. "I don't like that part," he says, in a half whisper. "Not that part."

"I am sorry," O'Connor says. What else is there to say?

The actor lifts his head, looking out and up, over the trees of his compound. The sky fills his eyes. He says, "I saw a girl . . ."

FLASHBACK 23

There's a party going on, in a house up in Big Sur. Big, rough-hewn log house cantilevered out over the cliff. Big, comfortable, big-roomed house full of Indian rugs and Mexican pottery and all *kinds* of dope. Big counterculture house with state-of-the-art stereo inside Shaker reproduction cabinets. Would you believe two platinum albums were *recorded* in this house? Of course you would.

Buddy had business up here, a little shmooze here and there. Somebody has to take care of the business end, make sure the IRS doesn't get *everything*. And he could take care of what had to be taken care of, and still kick back and party along the way. So he brought Jack. Jack doesn't get out of the compound much, doesn't do much of anything much, is not at *all* keeping himself in trim. Not at *all*.

Jack fell asleep. Early in the party, sun barely overhead, people grooving in the big room cantilevered out over the cliff, with the wall of plate-glass windows showing the whole fucking *ocean*, man, you can almost fucking see

Australia out there. And pine trees down both sides, furring the face of the cliff.

And Jack fell asleep. On a backless couch down at the end of the room, the foot of the couch against the big window, and that's where Jack fell asleep, his back against the glass, head against the glass, mouth hanging open, eyes closed, hands limp, nothing behind his poor befuddled head but the glass and the air and the sea and Australia. Just out of sight over there, beyond the glistening horizon.

The loud party noises—people yelling their conversations over the stereo sound of a not-yet-released new soft-rock album—did not wake Jack but seemed to soothe him, comfort him, convince him he was not alone, he was safe to slumber. But the first scream troubled his sleep, made him frown, made his mouth half close in protest.

The second scream dragged his eyes open. A blur of movement met him, a blur of sound blanketed his ears, and then voices became distinct, full of panic.

"She's freaked!"

"It's a bad trip!"

"Hold her, for Christ's sake!"

And the girl's voice, screaming, *"Get away! Get away!"*

Jack turned his wondering head and, along the line of windows, past the milling mob, he could see her, a skinny naked girl of fifteen or sixteen, ribs standing out below her breasts, face distorted, keeping a circle clear around herself by swinging a record jacket back and forth in wide swaths. She screamed and screamed, foam on her lips, and the people around her ducked and dodged, trying to reach her, trying to calm her, trying to get her under somebody's control.

Jack watched, and then somebody made a lunge for the girl, knocking the record jacket out of her hand. Her scream got louder, more shrill, and she spun about, eluding all those groping arms, and ran straight ahead, full speed through the window.

Jack turned his head, his cheek against the cool glass, and watched her go, in a long arc, out away from the building, high over the sea and the cliff, the shattered glass flying with her, gleaming like diamonds in the sun, the girl a skinny, wild-haired white spider flailing through the air, her scream filling the sky and rolling like Juggernaut through Jack's brain.

She fell so slowly, like a death in an arty Japanese movie, arcing out and down and out and down, the hard jewels of glass tumbling with her, and Jack watched her go, and saw the great bruised sea rise up for her, and he died. He breathed, he heard the sounds in the room, he saw the sunlight gleaming, he felt the glass warm against his cheek, but he died. The sea sucked the girl in, and he was dead.

Through the pandemonium of the room, Buddy shoved his way to Jack's side, grabbing him roughly by the elbow, saying urgently in his ear, "Dad! Get your shit together, dammit! We gotta get outa here!"

"Wendy," Jack whispered. His terror was so severe he couldn't move. He whispered, "Did you see her? Wendy?"

Buddy grabbed Jack's jaw in a tight and painful grip, turning Jack's face up toward his own hot angry glare. "Listen to me, you fucking asshole," Buddy said, low and fast, below the chaotic noises that had now overtaken the room behind him, but clear and ringing in Jack's ears. "I still need you," Buddy rasped, giving Jack's jaw a hard shake. "You do *not* freak out on me. You do *not* get found in this house where some underage cunt offed herself. You get up on your feet and you walk with me out of this house. You do it *now*."

"Buddy, Buddy," Jack said, brimming with gratitude, his eyes filling with tears, "where would I be without my Buddy? You're my oldest friend in all the world, do you know that?"

"Up, shit-for-brains," Buddy ordered him, and released Jack's jaw to grab his hand instead and twist his thumb painfully backward. "On your fucking *feet*."

"*You'll* save me, Buddy," Jack said, beginning to cry, struggling to rise from the couch, making it at last to the vertical, tottering there. "You'll save me, Buddy Buddy. You always save me, you always do."

"March," Buddy told him, twisting his thumb.

"It *was* Wendy," Jack whispered, shivering with dread, and the two old friends made their way out of that room and away from that party.

I'm so cold. I hurt all over. My thumb hurts, too, but that's something else. My jaw hurts, too, but that's something else. It's just that I'm so cold. Since I died, I'm cold a lot.

"What?" I say. Michael O'Connor has said something, but I was too cold to hear him.

So he repeats it. "Why did you call that girl Wendy?"

Wendy? What have I been saying? Something must have gone wrong, my balance isn't right, I'm not paying attention. *This cannot be.* I must be on guard, always on guard, and especially on guard with the media. Oh, my, yes. "Wendy?" I say, casually, lifting my head, thinking back. "That was the poor girl's name, I suppose."

"It was your *first* girl's name, too," he says.

Oh, damn you, Michael, you do have a memory between those ears, don't you? I smile at him. "Lots of Wendys in this old world," I say. "Anyway, it got covered up that we were there. Me and two other guys with . . . names."

"I don't remember anything about it," O'Connor says.

"You wouldn't," I assure him. "When a property is as

valuable as I am, a lot of very serious professional people see to it that nothing happens to lower that value. I am not a person anymore, you know, Michael, no, sir, not me. I am a *property*. A valuable property. A whole lot of people would be shit outa luck if anything happened to this property. So nothing does."

"Well, some things do," O'Connor suggests. "Some things did, anyway; you told me about them."

"But not anymore." I look around, at my domain. "I stay here now, mostly, since that time up at Big Sur. I make one picture a year now, that's all. I don't need to do any more; I don't need the money. I just have to do the one to keep myself current, part of the *scene*. Grandstanders, now, that's what I do. I don't, you know, *act* anymore. I could if I wanted, I still could, but it's hard, it's too hard, and who needs it? They don't pay their money to see me *become* somebody, not anymore. They pay to see me be *me*. An idealized *them*. I do clenched-jawline stuff a lot. I pick properties with *speeches* in them." I glower at Michael O'Connor: "You don't love me. You *never* loved me. You never loved *anybody*. You don't know *how* to love."

This speech seems to make O'Connor uncomfortable. He says, "But what about the talent? The gift?"

"Among my souvenirs."

"Well . . . what do you do with the rest of your time?" he asks. "The nine or ten months a year when you're not making a movie."

"I stay home," I say, smiling at the thought. "Right here. Anything I need, they bring me. I'm safe here." I smile at Michael, from my safety.

FLASHBACK 24

The naked giggling girl ran across the patio, past the pool, around the edge of the rose garden, and off across the rolling lawn. The naked Jack pursued her, gasping, grinning, dropping to his knees from time to time, struggling up again, lumbering on, following that round and muscular behind.

The girl had been told to see to it that Jack got his exercise, so that's what she was doing. When he got too close, she would dart away, laughing slightly, sticking her tongue out at him, wriggling a lot to encourage him. And when he would fall back, when he would seem to lose heart for the chase, she would slow, her looks would become seductive, her movements lewd, and slowly the light would come back into his eyes, his trembling limbs would firm themselves, and he would go on with the chase. Because, as they both knew, the other part of her instruction was that eventually he must catch her.

Out across the lawn she went. The distant high wall, which was topped by broken glass embedded in the cement, was barely visible through the surrounding layers of ornamental brush. Panting, grinning, eyes rolling, arms pumping, Jack followed, weaving from side to side, slowing, struggling, slowing, stopping, falling forward, landing on his face on the lush green lawn.

The girl ran on another few paces, her bright laughter rising toward the blue sky, but then she looked back and saw Jack lying there, face down, and she stopped, turned around, put her small fists on her lovely hips and considered the situation. A ruse? A temporary rest? But he wasn't moving, not at all, so finally she raised her voice and shouted toward the house, "He fell down!"

Immediately, the door in the end of the house beyond the multicar garage, the door leading to the security offices, opened and four young hefty men came trotting out. They all had short, military-style haircuts. All wore gray slacks, white shirts, narrow neutral ties, and beige or gray sports jackets. The four of them came trotting in unison across the lawn toward Jack as the naked girl also walked toward the unconscious man, wondering if her job here was finished now.

The security men reached Jack, flipped him over, checked him for vital signs, discussed the situation briefly with one another, and came to the conclusion this was no more than a normal kind of passing out, requiring no particular medical attention. Therefore, as the girl wandered away to get dressed, each of the four security men picked up one of Jack's limbs and carried him like a firemen's net across the lawn and through the main front door of the house.

Where Buddy was just coming down the main stairs, in a light gray summer suit, accompanied by two servants carrying his matched luggage. Hoskins, at the foot of the stairs to wish Mr. Pal bon voyage, became the hub of all motion, as Buddy and his entourage approached from above and Jack in the grip of his security quartet was borne in from without.

Hoskins gave his first attention to the conscious person, saying, "Enjoy your trip, sir."

His voice and manner grim, his cold eyes on Jack, Buddy said, "Oh, I will, Hoskins, believe me. I will."

"Yes, sir." Hoskins raised an eyebrow at the right front security man. "Yes?" he asked.

"No sweat," the security man said. "We'll just put him to bed."

"Bed," said the ghost of Jack, and smiled.

The security men made their way up the stairs with their burden. Buddy paused to watch them go, and the servants paused with him, carrying his bags. Jack and the security men reached the top of the stairs and disappeared on down the wide white hall. Buddy looked at Hoskins. He said, "Give Jack a message for me."

"Certainly, sir."

"Tell him," Buddy said, "not to kill himself before I get back."

Hoskins nodded, accepting receipt of the message. Buddy turned about and left, the servants trailing with his bags.

"That was six weeks ago," I say, feeling dreamier again. "When Buddy went away."

"And Buddy came home last night," O'Connor says.

This surprises and pleases me, and yet at the same time makes me nervous and scared. But why should I be nervous and scared? Buddy Pal is my oldest friend in all the world. "Gee, did he?" I ask. "Are you sure?"

"You talked with him last night."

"I did?" Wherever I look, there are deep black holes. "I can't remember," I say.

O'Connor leans forward. This is important to him, for some reason. "Try," he says.

I try, but it doesn't help. Sadness, sadness; all I can feel is sadness. I say, "I had a breakdown once, you know. Did I tell you?"

"You didn't tell me," O'Connor says, "but I do know. It was after Miriam Croft died."

Oh, I can feel that, live it again, those terrible moments in the back of the limousine, rushing across Connecticut. She was making such *noises*. I wanted her to stop making those awful *noises,* and then she did, and that was worse. *"Miriam!"* I screamed, trying to reach her, reach her, pull her back. *"Miriam, don't die! Don't die! Not you, too!"*

O'Connor's voice brings me back. He says, "Why did Miriam's death upset you so much? Why did it give you a nervous breakdown, so bad that after the funeral you had to be hospitalized for five months? The doctors told you you weren't to blame for her death, so what was there about it that affected you so strongly?"

"I don't know," I say. The nervousness is getting stronger. I don't want to talk anymore, I don't want to be *interviewed* anymore, I don't like the way this is going, I don't like any part of it. "I don't know," I say, "I don't know, I don't know."

"Could it be, Mr. Pine," O'Connor asks me, leaning over those huge gray knees of his, that nothing face pressing toward me, "could it be that it reminded you of something *earlier* in your life? Some other event, involving a woman, and death, and the backseat of a car?"

Rattled, my jaw trembling, I manage to say, "I don't know what you're talking about!"

"I think you do."

"No! I'm Jack Pine! I'm the movie star! I live here in this house and they take care of me! That's all there is! That's all there is!"

"Let's go back, Mr. Pine," O'Connor tells me, "to the very first time, your very first sexual experience with a woman."

Shaking my head, shaking my fists, I say, "I don't want to."

"You were so excited, you lost control," O'Connor says. "Do you remember telling me that? It was like an explosion, you said."

I cover my eyes with my hands, but still I can see. My whole body can see it now.

FLASHBACK 1A

Jack, sixteen years old, reared up over the waiting Wendy in the backseat of the car. His feet drummed against the door she'd just made him slam, switching out the light above his head. Wild-eyed, staring in the dark, his nose filled with a suffocating musk, he trembled all over, his body moving in rapid disorganized jerks. "I can't—" he cried, his voice breaking back to childish falsetto, "It's so— You're so—"

"Get *with* it, willya?" Wendy demanded, half laughing, teasing, poking at his chest with sharp-knuckled fingers. "Come *on*!"

Jack's arms flailed around. He beat himself on the head in his mad struggle to get control of himself. The Buddy-facade he'd come in here with had failed him and fled. Grabbing Wendy's shoulders in his fists, clutching tight, he yanked her this way and that, gibbering in frenzy, shaking her like Raggedy Ann.

"Jesus!" Wendy cried. "Watch it! Hey, the window crank! Look out, you're—What are you—*Gahhh!*"

Jack shook and thrust with rhythmic mania, flinging the

two of them about so that the car rocked on its springs, and down the road Buddy grinned to himself at the sound of it. But every time Jack lifted Wendy's body now, though in the darkness and in his own frenzy he didn't notice, her head merely flopped, back and forth on her shoulders.

"Yes!" Jack cried. "Yes! *Yes!*" And he collapsed atop her, gasping, shuddering all over, spent.

Slowly, at long last, he lifted himself again onto his elbows, perspiration glinting on his brow and his neck. "Wendy," he said, low and hoarse and still winded, "Wendy, I'll never forget you, I'll never—"

He stopped. He stared. His eyes bulged with horror. His scream filled the car like knives.

"I break things. I break things."

My lips are loose and blubbery, my eyes are crushed grapes, strings of foul seaweed hang down in my throat, my head is a cavern full of crows, every nerve and sinew in my entire body is untied and aching and trembling. I am like the body of someone who has been electrocuted. This is what it feels like afterward, after the lightning has filled your body and done its work. "Punish me!" I cry. "Punish me!"

I stare from my bleeding eyes and O'Connor is there, still there, always there. He's plagued me my entire life long. "But you can't punish me," I tell him. "I'm a property. I'm too valuable to punish. Nobody can touch me."

"Buddy helped you that night, didn't he?" O'Connor asks.

"I don't want to talk anymore."

"You've come this far," he says. "Buddy helped you get rid of Wendy's body. That's why he's always had such a

206

hold over you, why you could never refuse him anything he wanted. Why you've always been grateful to him, and always afraid of him."

"He's my-me-my-my old-old-old—"

"It was Buddy, wasn't it, who thought of what to do that night?"

Yes, I think, while my mouth wallows and drools, sloppy, piggish, revolting . . . Yes, I think. I nod.

FLASHBACK 1B

Jack trembled and was useless, nearly dropping the girl's body, but Buddy was strong. He held her ankles in the crook of one arm, opening the trunk of the car with his other hand, while Jack blubbered and shook, his arms around the girl's stiffening thickening body under the armpits. Already she felt different, heavier and more animal and less real. Already she was less real.

"I always break things," Jack blubbered.

"You get too excited, Dad," Buddy told him, the trunk lid rising like a mouth opening. "You got to learn to take it easy."

Jack moaned. He stood there sobbing and moaning while Buddy eased her legs into the trunk and then had to unclamp Jack's hands to make him let go of her torso. Buddy stuffed her into the trunk, pushed her hair in after, turned her so the lid would close, slammed the lid. "I'll drive," he said.

Jack just stood there, his head shaking, mouth working, shoulders sagging, arms hanging limply at his side. Buddy gazed at him with contempt, then deliberately kicked him on the shin. "Ow!" Jack said, and stared at Buddy wide-eyed.

"Get in the car," Buddy told him. "Front, passenger side."

Jack obeyed, and Buddy got behind the wheel and started the engine. Jack said, in a tiny voice, "What are we going to do, Buddy?"

"Get rid of it," Buddy said, and backed the car around in a half circle.

"We don't go to the police?"

"Never!" Buddy shifted into park and looked at his friend. "You want to go to prison? Come out when you're thirty-six?"

"No, Buddy."

"You can go to the cops now," Buddy told him, "or never. You don't change your mind tomorrow. You don't change your mind *ever*."

"Yes, Buddy."

"Which is it?"

"I don't want to go to prison," Jack said. He was very humble, as though he were talking to God, and God was impatient with him.

"So it's no cops," Buddy said. "Is that right? Just to get things straight."

"No cops, Buddy," Jack said.

"Okay," Buddy said, and shifted into drive, and took them away from there.

Out on the highway, Jack said, humbly, "Why are you doing this for me, Buddy?"

"I'm your best friend," Buddy said. He was paying attention to the traffic and the speed limit. He didn't want to get stopped by a highway patrolman.

"You are my best friend, Buddy," Jack said.

Buddy laughed. "And it's a movie!" he said.

They left the highway where the signs pointed for the lake, then turned off that road and climbed high to another place where lovers sometimes liked to come. But none were here tonight.

The road made a sharp turn to the right. Ahead, a wide dirt parking area narrowed on the left side to a cliff, with the lake far below, glinting cold in the starlight.

"Open the windows and get out," Buddy said.

Jack did it and came around to the driver's side, where Buddy was wedging a rock onto the accelerator, making the engine roar. Jack said, "What's happening, Buddy?"

"That ought to do it," Buddy said, and straightened. The engine roared as though it were afraid. Buddy said, "Wendy always said she'd run away from home. So she did. Stole her old man's car and ran."

Jack's jaw trembled, his eyes filled with tears. "She was so nice," he said.

"She was a sicko," Buddy said. "Say good-bye to her, if you want."

Jack moved back to the trunk of the car, remembering how Wendy had looked when he'd first opened the car door and the light had gone on, and there she was. And now . . .

The engine roar was like screaming. It made the car vibrate; it seemed to heave. Buddy had left the lights on, and the red and white lights reflected from the enigmatic trunk and the gleaming bumper chrome. Jack reached his hand out toward the trunk, wishing with such intensity that it broke his heart, wishing it all undone.

"Here goes," Buddy said. He reached in through the open driver's door to shift to drive.

screams, screaming, engine roars, flashing lights in red and white reflecting from the bumper chrome, slicking on the heaving trunk of the car, madness, danger, movement, peril, speed . . .

I feel so empty. I feel like a tree after the sap has been drained away. Big, woody, stupid, dull tree, too dumb to fall over. My eyes are open, but I see nothing. Even my forehead can't see anymore. Hearing how dull my voice is, hearing how I'm a tree and I'm empty but there's no echo, hearing how even the echo is drained out of me, I say, "Nobody ever knew about that, except Buddy and me."

"And gradually," the voice says, "the memory faded. Nobody linked you to Wendy's disappearance, you got so you could sleep at night again, Buddy's strength carried you through."

"Buddy never mentioned it again, not once."

"Buddy didn't have to mention it."

"No," I say. "That's right."

"Still," the voice says, "time went by, and everything was all right. You were going to be okay. But then it happened again."

"Yes," I say.

"It wasn't your fault this time," the voice says, "but the ingredients were the same. Sex. The woman. The backseat of the car. And she was dead."

"Miriam. Don't die."

"But she did. And you had your breakdown."

"I could never weave those goddamn baskets."

"And when you came out of the hospital at last," the voice says, "you were still terrified of women. You believed you were doomed to destroy them, not wanting to. That's why you tried that interlude with George Castleberry."

"Also," I am forced to say, "Biff Novak was a great part."

The voice ignores that. Unstoppable, the voice rolls on: "And since then, you have been attracted only to strong women, too strong for you to hurt. And when they hurt you, as eventually they did, you felt you deserved it, because of Wendy."

"Did I?" I am surprised to find that I am capable of surprise. "Maybe I did," I say, and realize that one of these days I must rethink all my relationships. But not just at this particular moment.

"It was the girl who went out the window at Big Sur," the voice says, "who brought it all back for you yet again."

So different, and yet the same. The same arcing fall, reaching out and down, so slow and then so fast, plummeting toward the water. The car in the night, its lights on, dropping toward its own illuminated reflection in the still, deep lake. The girl in the sunlight amid the jewels of broken glass, dropping toward the hungry roiling sea. The same. Wendy. Dead again. "It keeps happening," I say. "No matter what I do, it keeps happening."

"After Big Sur," the voice says, "you withdrew to this estate."

"I'm safe here."

"You almost never leave," the voice says. It knows so much about me, this wonderful voice. It knows so much, and it stays so calm. If *I* knew that much about me, I wouldn't stay calm. Oh, boy. You couldn't *get* me calm, if

I knew all that. And the voice goes calmly on, saying, "You keep yourself drugged—"

"Mellowed. Mellowed."

"It's been hurting your career, Mr. Pine," the voice says. "Buddy didn't like that."

FLASHBACK 25

The room to the right of the front entrance, a large square pleasant place with views of the lawn and main drive, had been turned into an office. Desks, filing cabinets, library table, computer, shelves filled with scripts and stationery supplies; it might have been a Midwestern insurance agency. Jack himself rarely entered this room, his interest in the mundane details of real life being minimal at best, but today his drifting took him without particular plan or purpose through just another doorway, and there he was, in the office.

And there was his secretary, clipping things from newspapers and magazines and mounting them in the clear plastic folder-pages of an album. And there was Buddy, seated at the library table by the windows, going over ledgers with Sol, the accountant, a short, wide, ugly man with a brain like a Renaissance Italian. Buddy and Sol were both looking grim, which Jack wasn't likely to notice. In fact, looking around with pleased surprise to see where his drift had led him, he said, "Ah. My merry staff. My merry accountant. My merry Buddy. How is everybody?"

"Good morning, Jack," the secretary said, glancing up briefly from her work, her manner neutral.

The accountant, squinting at Jack across the ledgers, said, "Jack, if you have a minute—"

"Sol," Buddy said, placing a hand on the accountant's forearm on the table, "let me talk to him."

The accountant shrugged. "Just so somebody does," he said.

Jack's smile turned vague but didn't disappear. Buddy got to his feet, crossed the room, took Jack by the elbow, and said, "Let's go for a walk, Dad."

"Sure, Buddy."

They left the office, Buddy holding on to Jack's elbow, went out the front door, walked across the lawn, and made their way to the formal rose garden at the side of the house, where two gardeners puttered, accomplishing very little. Buddy looked at them. "Vamos," he said.

They vamosed. Jack smiled after them, smiled at the roses, smiled at Buddy. "It's nice here," he said.

"Dad," Buddy said, "we're in trouble."

"Take some blues, Buddy," Jack advised him. "Don't let it get you down. Knock back a little T and B."

"We're beyond that, Dad," Buddy said. He gave Jack's elbow one little shake and released him. "Sol tells me we're spending ahead of income," he said. "We've got investments out there, they need cash, we've got to prime the pump, and we don't have it."

Uncaring, still with that same vague smile, Jack said, "All goes to the candy man."

"A lot of it does," Buddy agreed. "Dad, you hurt yourself in the industry with that Academy Award mess, and now you're hurting your career. You're making bad choices."

"Buddy, Buddy," Jack said, reaching for his buddy but missing, "loosen up. What does it matter?"

"It matters a lot," Buddy told him. "All you care about is to stay stoned and to stay right here inside these walls."

"Come on, Buddy, I go out."

"Where?"

Jack thought. "Brazil," he said.

"Once a year." Buddy shook his head in disgust. "You're turning into Howard Hughes," he said, "only you don't have any tool company. You still have to make a living, but you don't want to anymore."

"Kick back, Buddy, kick back."

But Buddy stayed tense and serious. "We built something nice here, Dad," he said, "and I'm not gonna let you pull it down."

With mild curiosity, Jack said, "Whatcha gonna do, Buddy?"

"Stop you," Buddy said.

"That was just before Buddy left on his trip," the voice says, "six weeks ago."

Focus. Focus. Something's scaring me, something's wrong here, and it is necessary for me right *now* to get under control, find the reins of my existence, gather myself together into one place. Mayday! Mayday! Battle stations! Prepare to crash dive!

No; prepare to crash surface. Up out of the depths, all in one piece, coming up to the real world, blinking around. And if I see my shadow?

I see O'Connor. Ah-hah; I'd lost that. O'Connor. The interview. For a while there it was just a voice, almost inside my head with me. I was in a Beckett play all by myself, me and the voice. Saying . . .

Wait a minute. *That's* what's wrong. "Wait a minute," I say, looking at O'Connor, seeing O'Connor plain. "You aren't from *People*."

"No, sir," he says, "I'm not."

"Damn straight," I tell him, sitting up more firmly, converting my fear into righteous rage. "*People* wouldn't

217

put all this stuff in; dead girls in trunks of cars, sleeping with George." Suddenly I get it; I stare at him, wide-eyed. "The *National Enquirer*!"

"Sir, I—"

Alarmed and outraged, I tell him, "Pal, I don't talk to the *Enquirer*! I set the *dogs* on the *Enquirer*!" Lifting my head, I cry, "Hoskins!"

And he appears, as is his function. Bowing from the waist, my unflappable Hoskins says, "You bellowed, sir?"

Good man. I say to him, "Hoskins, do we got any dogs?"

"No, sir," Hoskins says.

"Drat," I say. It would have been fun to watch this bland and boring O'Connor high-tailing it across the lawn, pen and notebook flying, pursued by slavering dogs. I say, "Well, we got security men, Hoskins, you can't deny that."

"I do not deny it, sir," he says.

"Send me security men," I tell him. "Sadistic security men, with a history of psychopathology. We got here a *National Enquirer* reporter, and I— "

"Oh, I think not, sir," Hoskins says.

I frown at him. Hoskins thinks *not*? What does this mean? "What does this mean, Hoskins?"

But it's O'Connor who answers me, saying, "It means I'm not from the *National Enquirer*, Mr. Pine. I'm not a journalist at all."

What's this? I'm chatting with some bum in off the street? I say, "Then what are you doing talking to me? You got an appointment?"

"Sir," he says, smooth and calm as ever, "as I told you at the beginning of the interrogation—"

"Interview," I say, correcting him in a hurry, feeling a sudden alarm.

"Interrogation," he says, and then it gets worse. "The other police officers," he says, "read you your rights and explained the situation to you before you came out of the house. If you don't remember that, I'm sorry, but"—and he smiles, faintly—"the legalities have been preserved."

All I can do is stare at him. "You're a *cop*?"

"Detective Second Grade Michael O'Connor," he says. "Bel Air police."

"But—But—" My mind is swirling, I can't *believe* this is happening. I say, "It was an accident! It was twenty-five years ago, I didn't mean to kill her, it was an accident! Besides, I, I've been a useful member of society ever since, I've *paid* my debt to society, I—I gave, I give—Hoskins!"

He's right there, of course. "Sir?" he says.

"Every Christmas," I say, because I need him to vouch for me now, I need Hoskins on my side now, "every Christmas, don't we, we give, we send out those UNICEF cards, don't we?"

"Yes, sir," Hoskins says.

I face O'Connor—policeman O'Connor—I face him and spread my hands. "See?"

"Mr. Pine," this policeman— policeman!—says, "it isn't a twenty-five-year-old felony that concerns us now. Let's talk about last night."

Feeling scared again, nervous and scared, covering it with mulishness, I say, "I don't remember last night. I wasn't here. I was in a different galaxy."

"Maybe we can bring it back for you," O'Connor says.

"No need," I say. "Don't trouble yourself."

"No trouble," he assures me. "It was late last evening. You were coming down the main staircase. The front door opened and Buddy Pal walked in. Do you remember that?"

"No," I say, though in fact faint images are rising to the surface of my brain, little bubbles of image, each with a picture inside, each bubble popping, the images staying behind, filling in, bit by bit.

"Think back," O'Connor tells me. "Buddy Pal walked in. You said something like, 'Hi, Buddy. Where've you been?' Do you remember that?"

"Maybe," I say. "What's wrong with that? What difference does it make?"

"What did he answer?"

"What?"

"When you asked me him where he'd been," O'Connor

says, patiently pressing me, holding me, squeezing me, "when you asked him where he'd been, what did he say?"

Why should I cooperate with this son of a bitch? "I don't know," I say.

"Think," O'Connor suggests.

"I don't remember."

"Think."

I think. I can't help it. I think more than I should. I try not to think, I do all kinds of things to stop from thinking, but none of them ever work, not for long. I think, and then Buddy's remembered voice comes into my mind, and I repeat what he'd said to me, where he'd been: "Brazil," I say.

O'Connor nods. "Is it coming back now?"

It is, dammit. Not thinking is hard to do. "I was already stoned when Buddy walked in, but when I saw him, when I saw what had happened, what he'd *done*, I right away took a lot more stuff."

FLASHBACK 26

The east parlor by night, in the glow of its table lamps, was a warm and gentle room, cozy and comforting and good. Now, on the table where Dr. Ovoid had spread his samples, there stood a large Limoges plate bearing two parallel white lines of powder. Jack bent over this table, his back to the doorway, where Buddy stood watching him. One end of a straw was stuck into Jack's nostril. His head moved from left to right across the plate, using the straw to vacuum up one of the two lines. Then he turned and looked at Buddy, his expression dulled, but with terror showing through.

Buddy smiled, with his new face. "Go ahead, Dad," he said, still sounding like Buddy. "Get it on."

Still sounding like Buddy. But not looking like Buddy. Looking like *Jack*. The doctors in Brazil had taken that similarity of feature and bone structure, had combined that with their own high skills and techniques, and had turned Buddy into a new Jack.

A better Jack. A healthier Jack, thinner and trimmer. A Jack who might have come into existence in the normal way, except that the original had led his body down other avenues. But here he was, as he might have been.

Jack turned away from that cold-eyed other self. He inhaled the second line, and behind him Buddy stepped further into the room. Jack remained bent over the table, staring at the bare plate, trying to see himself in it, trying to see the real self reflected in the plate, but seeing nothing.

Buddy's old voice said, "You know what this means, don't you?"

Jack tried a quick grin at the plate, but the feeling of it on his face was so terrible he stopped at once. He said, "It means I'm temporarily insane."

"It means, Dad," Buddy said, "you're permanently retired."

Slowly Jack turned, losing his balance briefly, pressing his hand to the smooth warm surface of the table. Fearfully he looked at Buddy—that face!—and said, "Buddy, what have you done?"

"You can *see* what I've done," Buddy said, gesturing at his new face. "The question is, what am I going to do now? Can you guess?"

"No," Jack said.

"Sure you can," Buddy told him, grinning Jack's famous crooked grin. "You just don't want to. Because you know what I'm going to do is take your place."

"You're crazy!" Jack yelled. "You can't take my place! You can't possibly take my place!"

Buddy shook his—Jack's—head. "An eight-by-ten glossy photograph could come damn near taking your place," he said, "the way you've been recently. Don't worry about me making it work, Dad, this has been very carefully thought out."

"You'll never get away with it!" Jack cried. "People will know!"

"People?" Buddy asked. "What people?"

"Irwin! My agent, Irwin! You think you can fool *him*?"

"He's in on it," Buddy told him. "Your accountant, Sol, is in on it."

Appalled, Jack staggered back against the table. "I don't believe you."

Buddy was inexorable. "A whole lot of people make their living off you, Dad," he said, "and you're putting all of our livelihoods at risk. Something had to be done."

With a mad laugh, breaking into falsetto, Jack cried, "You don't *sound* like me!"

Buddy smiled—Jack's smile! When he spoke, his sound and intonations were very like Jack's; not perfect, but a very good imitation, about on a par with a nightclub mimic. "I've been seeing a voice coach," said this new manner. "We aren't there yet, but we'll make it." With his own original voice, Buddy added, "And just to make things easier, next month you're going into Cedars of Lebanon for an adenoid operation. We've already made the reservation. Don't worry, you'll be on the celeb eighth floor." Reverting to the Jack imitation, he said, "Somehow, your voice will never be exactly the same again. But you'll carry on. The public will be proud of you."

"I don't believe this," Jack said, staring at the pattern in the carpet. "A conspiracy."

"Too much money involved, Dad," the new face said in the new voice. "This was the only solution."

"But—" Jack squinted at Buddy as though that new face were a glaring searchlight, difficult to look at. "What happens to *me*?" he demanded, trying to sound tough but with the terror peeking through.

"You become a bigger star than ever," the Buddy/Jack said.

"No, dammit," the original Jack cried, fear so distorting his face that he looked less like himself. "You know what I mean!" Slapping his chest, he cried, "Me! *This* me!"

Buddy/Jack chuckled. "Dr. Ovoid has a nice sanitarium up the coast—"

"*He's* in it, too? My *doctor*?"

"He'll make you feel good every day for the rest of your life," Buddy/Jack said. "You won't mind at all. It's the way you want to live anyway."

223

"You—" Jack moved from side to side, his feet shuffling on the intricately designed carpet. "You've taken everything," he said. "My lighter, my money, my sweaters, my car. My *wives*."

"I never did get into Lorraine," Buddy/Jack said, with a little grin. "My one great regret."

"And now," Jack said, moving, shuffling, staring, "now you want my *life*."

His true contempt showing through fully at last, Buddy/Jack said, "I'm a much better you than you could ever be."

A stink of truth in that statement twisted Jack's features, made him turn away, stagger across the room, toward the broad white mantelpiece. But then he changed, he found his equilibrium and his selfhood, he fought back. Spinning around, triumphant, aggressive, he pointed at the poor mannequin, the second-rate Buddy/Jack, and shouted, "You don't have my *talent*!"

Buddy/Jack's Jack-mouth twisted in scorn. "*You* don't have your talent," he said, "not anymore. You haven't had it for five years. You *used* to be an actor, one of the best, but now you're just a star turn. You go in front of the camera, you do your Jack Pine number, all the little schticks and tics, the shoulder movements and the grins, all those bits of business you developed over the years to take the place of working on the character. You do all that shit, and you come off. *That* I can do."

Oscar stood on the mantle. The golden statuette, the highest award an actor can receive, the acknowledgement of excellence from his peers. Jack spun about, grabbed up Oscar, held him like a flaming torch aloft, and cried, "Then why do I have *this*?"

Buddy/Jack chuckled; a Jack schtick. "In honor of your farewell performance," he said.

"Nooo!!" Jack screamed, and rushed forward, Oscar raised high above his head.

I stare in horror at O'Connor, seeing those fragmentary memories, disbelieving them. "I couldn't!" I cry. "Not with Oscar!"

O'Connor reaches behind him and brings out an object. "Do you recognize this, Mr. Pine?" he asked.

It is Oscar. He is beaten and battered and bloodstained. His head is bent down onto his chest as though he's dead.

And now the memory comes clear: myself, manic, laughing, striking downward over and over at that creature in the middle of the carpet. And I can hear myself screaming, "*My* face? Not *my* face, you don't take *my* face!" And beating and beating at that face which will never be me, never, never.

And stopping. Panting, gleefully grinning, staring down at him, saying, "*Now* you don't look like me." And it is true. He doesn't look like me anymore. In fact, he doesn't look much like anybody anymore.

"Oh, God," I say now, in the sunlight, and cover my eyes, not wanting to see poor Oscar there. "I killed him," I say.

"Yes," O'Connor said. "Buddy Pal is dead."

"Oh, him," I say, distracted. "I meant Oscar." I look at O'Connor, trying not to see poor Oscar. "But Buddy really is dead, isn't he?"

"Yes," O'Connor says. "And after you killed him . . ."

FLASHBACK 27

Manic, wired, Jack emerged quietly from the main front door of the house and walked around toward the garage. When he was almost there, a security man approached him out of the darkness, saying, "Everything all right, Mr. Pine?"

Jack screamed in surprise and shock, then recovered, gabbled a second, and at last said, "What? All right? Of course everything's all right. Naturally everything's all right. Why wouldn't everything be all right?"

"No reason, sir," the security man said.

"I'm just going for a little drive, that's all," Jack said, straining to act, to *perform*, naturalness and calm. "Be off with you now," he said, as though casually. "Go on to bed."

"I'm supposed to patrol down here, Mr. Pine," the security man said.

"I don't *want* you to patrol!" Jack snapped at him. "I'm the boss around here, and if I don't want you to patrol you don't patrol!"

"Yes, sir," the security man said.

"I don't *need* patrols!" Jack yelled. "Not tonight! Look how nice everything is! It's the full moon!"

"Yes, sir," the security man said.

"Go to bed, or you're fired!"

"Good night, sir," the security man said.

The security man went away. Jack went on to the garage, opened the first door, went inside, and a minute later backed out the Mercedes. Giggling at the wheel, he backed the Mercedes in a great loop, off the drive and over the lawn and through the roses and right up to the wall of the house, stopping directly in front of an east parlor window, the rear bumper of the car just touching the wall of the house.

Jack climbed out from behind the wheel, went to the rear of the car, opened the trunk. Then he went around the car, slipping at one point, falling to his knees, recovering, using the front of the car to brace himself so he could stand again, then hurrying on.

He went back through the front door, down the long hall, and into the east parlor, where the *thing* lay on the floor, drying blood in random blobs and lines disrupting the intricate pattern of the carpet. Jack stepped over the *thing* and opened the window and looked out at the rear of the Mercedes, the open trunk just below him. "Good," he muttered, grinning. "Still there. Good."

He went back to the *thing* on the floor, grabbed it by the wrists, dragged it across the floor. The mess in the room he could take care of tomorrow. Every other problem could be taken care of tomorrow. There was only one thing that absolutely and positively had to be dealt with tonight.

And Jack knew how to deal with it.

"I was doing it *again* last night," I say, remembering now at last, in awe of that previous self, that mad, busy, energetic, straining, scheming previous self. "All over again."

"That's right, Mr. Pine," O'Connor says. "You followed the same method for disposing of the body as you did so many years ago with Wendy. You stuffed the body in the trunk of the car."

"Yes. I remember."

"Wendy's final resting place was deep water."

"The lake."

"You dropped her there, in her father's car, from high on a cliff."

"Yes."

"That was the pattern you repeated last night."

I rub my face with both hands. I'm so tired. No matter what you do, you can never do enough. I say, "I still only get bits and pieces of it. I was so stoned last night, I couldn't . . . I don't even know how I got home."

"Oh, you had no trouble," O'Connor says, mysteriously.

But there's another mystery, I suddenly realize. Sitting up straighter, frowning at O'Connor, I say, "Wait a minute. I was wasted. I don't remember a thing. And nobody else was there. If I dumped Buddy and the car in the ocean, how come *you* know all about it?"

"Because it wasn't the ocean, Mr. Pine," he tells me. "You're right, you were very heavily influenced by drugs last night."

"Not the ocean? But—" I try to remember. I get bits of it, all so similar to Wendy: the car heaving in neutral with the weight on the accelerator, the gleaming Mercedes trunk in the bright moonlight, the moonlight sparkling off the water far below . . . "It's all there," I say, trying to piece it together. "Car—water—edge of the cliff— "

"Edge, all right," O'Connor says, "but not of any cliff. And in the state you were in, you couldn't tell one body of water from another. Besides, you do hate to leave the property."

Hate to leave the property? No trouble getting home? For the first time today, I turn full about and look over at the swimming pool.

Frogmen and scuba divers are standing there, beside the pool. Something lies on the lawn under a sheet. A police-department wrecker, its back to the pool, is slowly winching my beautiful Mercedes back up onto dry land.

The Mercedes. In the swimming pool.

I look at O'Connor. "Did I really do that?" I say.

"Yes, sir."

What could I say? "Silly me," I said

O'Connor gets to his feet, putting his pen and notepad away, smoothing out the gray knees of his trousers. "Shall we go, Mr. Pine?" he asks.

Hoskins bows toward me. "Shall I pack your bag, sir?"

I look again at the Mercedes, then at O'Connor. "Good idea, Hoskins," I say.

"For how long a stay, sir?"

"Oh, about twelve years, Hoskins, I would guess."

"Very good, sir. May I help you to your feet?"

"Excellent, Hoskins."

He helps me to my feet. I modestly close the robe about myself. Glancing over at the pool, I remember something else; too late. "I forgot to get my lighter back," I say.

"Ready, Mr. Pine?" asks O'Connor.